Chasing the Crown

Kail Harbick

Chasing the Crown Written by Kail Harbick

Editor-in-Chief: Steve William Laible

Cover concept & design: Melissa Norlund

Formatted for publication: Melissa Norlund

FIRST EDITION

Published by THE KODEL GROUP, LLC (TKG)

PO BOX 38 Grants Pass, Oregon 97528

To contact the author, illustrator, editors or publisher

Email: kailharbick@yahoo.com

Email: info@kodelgroup.com

The characters and events in this book are fictional and products of the author's imagination and any resemblance to actual persons or events is coincidental.

ISBN   978-1-62485-006-6

Library of Congress Cataloging -in -Publication Data

Harbick, Kail.

 Chasing the Crown: a novel / Kail Harbick — 1st edition.

ISBN   978-1-62485-006-6

1.Women—Fiction. 2. Pageants—Fiction. 3. Oregon—Fiction .

4.Marital Conflict—Fiction.

Library of Congress Control Number: 2012944814

Printed in the United States of America

Mom, you were there for me from the first letter, of the first word, of the first chapter to the last two words of the book…The End.

You were there for me from the first, to the one hundredth and one rewrite, and that is no hyperbole.

Morning and night for over three years, we laughed and cried with "Lucy" as we edited my book. Thank You! Thank you, for caring and loving the characters as much as I do. I will surely miss our time…'till the next one.

I could have never written this novel without you. Your name, Karen Curtis, should be on the cover with mine…I'm just saying.

I love you.

Acknowledgments

My loving husband, Darin, thank you for all your support.

My children, Tyler, Trey and Taya, I am proud of each of you.

My first editor, Karen Curtis, nobody will ever see my first drafts, but you. I don't care what all the writers say; "do" show your work to your mother! Mom, you're the best.

Ed Curtis, I love you, and Dad thanks for listening to Mom talk about my book … every day!

Thanks to my two brothers and their wives, Colby and Heather Curtis and Keene and Jodi Curtis. I wish we lived closer.

Melissa Norlund, who made sure I stayed true to my voice and true to "Lucy", thank you for crossing the finish line with me.

Ceil Schwalbach your pageantry expertise in those early years were invaluable to me.

Louise Harbick, more than a sister-in-law—my daily running mate, friend, and confidant.

Teresa Harbick, always a friend.

Special thanks to Steve Laible and his excellent TKG publishing team.

Philip Alan, your eye captures all things beautiful. For more photos please visit. philipalanphotography.com

Kathleen "Moosie" Fowler, your support is appreciated.

To the women who participated under my pageant directorship, thank you for the memories and the muse for this novel.

~ONE~
At First You Dream

The miserable weekend began Friday afternoon. The front door banged behind Adam, my fifth-grade son. The thud of his backpack hitting the floor interrupted my favorite show, *The Young and the Restless*. Jake and Suzy ran past him to their bedrooms.

"Mom!"

"Pick that up, please." I set my crochet project on the coffee table. Only nine rows were left of the last scarf to make number ten for the soldiers overseas.

"My teacher's making me do a family photo tree. I need pictures, lots of pictures, especially of Grandma and Grandpa Rupp." Adam bent over, digging through his backpack and brought out a crumpled piece of paper, waving it in the air. Hearing Adam refer to his dad's deceased parents warmed my heart.

Adam dropped the paper on my lap. Scanning his homework, it was clear his teacher had assigned a big project for us to complete.

I tucked the military green scarf back into the canvas bag. "When is it due?"

"Monday." Adam grabbed his pack and skipped through the kitchen toward his bedroom.

"Monday?" I smoothed the wrinkles of the crumpled assignment. "This is dated a week ago and you are just giving it to me now?" I almost pulled him back to sit him down to start on his homework, but I knew the kids were hungry and Tom would be home in twenty minutes, starving. There was just enough time to prepare dinner. Macaroni and cheese with hot dogs and the all-important-vegetable, green beans, would have to do.

"Tonight we'll fill in the names on the branches of the family tree. Saturday night I'll find the matching photos and Sunday we'll put it all together. So no video games for you, son, for the next three nights."

Adam groaned from his bedroom.

The next evening Adam and I discussed the family tree project while Tom settled into his favorite chair and kicked up his feet to watch the news. During commercials he rested his eyelids, until eventually he was softly snoozing.

Adam, with the attention span of a typical ten-year old, couldn't stop yawning. I tucked him, Jake and Suzy into their beds.

In the spare bedroom I searched for the old, family photos. Boxes were piled high. *What a mess.* I turned off the bright ceiling light and turned on a nightstand lamp, which was sitting on a plastic crate. To let the stale air out, I opened the window. The cool, fresh air had been missed from this particular room for much, much too long.

Dust scattered as I lifted the lids from shoeboxes. No photos. I stood, hands on hips and wondered where to look next. The folded high chair and playpen in front of the open closet, where my wedding gown still hung, sparked fond memories. Memories of those early years—marriage and then babies—I smiled.

I picked my way through boxes of old toys, out-of-style shoes and clothes, and books. I shoved memorabilia and holiday decorations to the other side of the room. Taking a deep breath, I wondered when I would get organized.

I swiped my finger through the dust on Tom's mother's dresser in the corner. As I opened the drawers, the scent of stale lavender was still present, after all of these years.

There it was, in the last drawer, the shoebox I was looking for. I squeezed into the only available space on the floor and sat with my back up against the wall. The dust made me sneeze. The first photo on top of the stack hadn't seen light in what must have been a decade. Squinting to look closer, it was of me holding Adam on my hip, his legs wrapped around my waist. We were both so young.

Sorting through the old photos, one by one, I looked for the most interesting pictures for Adam's school project…pictures of family…pictures of pets…pictures of vacations. I forced myself to stay on task. Someday I'll stick these photos into an album.

One picture stopped me. Tom and I stood arm-in-arm on the beach. I pulled the photo closer to admire my favorite hairstyle from years gone by. Mindlessly I ran my fingers through my stringy, unkempt hair. In the picture, I was golden tan, fit, and sexy wearing *Daisy Dukes* and a blue bikini top.

I looked again at the pretty woman in the photo. *Where had that person gone?* I leaned my head back and stared blankly at the ceiling. *I'd lost myself.* A depression headache hovered. My self-esteem snapped like a dry, brittle stick. The pictures in the shoebox revealed the truth. I had vanished.

I brushed at the tear rolling down my cheek and looked at the next photo. I studied my figure, curves in all the right places, firm legs, and strong arms. Why hadn't I appreciated how athletic I was? I tried to blank out my thoughts, but they persisted. I turned the picture over. On the bottom right corner, a photo stamp dated just over ten years ago.

Back then I could run thirteen miles and it felt like a stroll to the corner market and back. I had even placed third in a half-marathon. Glancing at the tarnished trophy shoved on the shelf in the closet, I swallowed a sad sob. Now I couldn't even run up thirteen stairs without struggling to breathe.

"Lucy?" Tom stood in his boxers and T-shirt, staring at me.

I forced a yawn to hide the tears that grieved for the girl in the photo, who no longer existed.

"It's late, Lucy. Midnight. How much longer?" Tom reached out his hand to pull me up.

I ignored his gesture. "Another fifteen minutes. I'm almost finished."

Tom nodded and turned toward our bedroom.

I cleared my throat. "Tom, do you still think I'm pretty?" He took his time, before turning back toward me. I waited for his answer.

During those early years, Tom told me almost every day how beautiful I was. He'd give me a sideways glance with his dark eyes and say, "You are D.D.G."

I would giggle, place my hand on my hip, and ask, "Why am I alive, if I'm drop dead gorgeous?" Even during those moments, when I held Adam on my hip, while pregnant with Jake, my husband could always find something sweet to say.

Tom studied me. "What's this all about, Lu?"

"I was just wondering…"

Tom wove through the boxes, knelt and placed a finger under my chin. He lifted my face. "Lucy, don't be ridiculous. Of course, I think you're gorgeous." He said a little too quickly, with a hint of humor and a smile, and kissed my forehead. "Come to bed. We have a busy day tomorrow. Church, you know."

"Alright, I'll be there in fifteen. I'm almost done gathering Adam's photos." After Tom left, I looked again at the picture in my hand. Tom's nonchalant answer chipped at my heart.

I placed the lid back on the shoebox and made my way to join Tom who was already asleep. Out of habit, I wrapped myself around his warm body and slid my feet between his legs, but sleep didn't come. Thoughts ran rampant. *What happened to the girl in the photograph? Would I ever find her again?*

As sure as Sunday is the first day of the week, I knew the telephone ringing was Tom's sister, Claudia. I groaned and slid deeper under the flannel sheet. I rolled over and peeked. Illuminated orange dots formed numbers that glared back at me.

"Oh, no! 8:23." Panic zipped through my body like a lightning bolt. I burst out of bed, wiggled into my pink robe, grabbed the telephone, and ran down the hallway. "Hello, Claudia."

"Sleep in again, Lucy?" She sounded too cheery for an early Sunday morning.

"Nice guess. I'm running behind and need to get breakfast for the kids." I slipped through the living room where the kids, still in pajamas, fought over the afghan while watching Sunday morning cartoons.

"Kids, turn that down. I can't hear," I hollered, dashing to the kitchen.

Claudia rambled on, oblivious to my frenzied morning. "I was hoping Tom, the kids and you might skip the service at your church this morning and attend my church. Today we—"

I held back another groan. "Sorry, Claudia. We're happy with our church." I turned back toward the living room and motioned to the three cherubs to scoot off the couch and get ready for Sunday school.

"What do you have against our church, Lucy? After all, Tom and I grew up in that church. Besides you drive past it and go on for miles to yours."

I'd heard this all before. I gave my sister-in-law the same answer as last Sunday when she asked. "The kids' best friends attend our church. They love their teacher. Listen Claudia, I gotta go. Thanks for the invite." I ended the conversation before she started another sentence.

I stepped into the living room, where the kids were still sprawled on the couch. "Your dad should be here just one Sunday morning to help me get you kids moving," I muttered, still fuming about Tom's older sister's annoying phone call. Back in the kitchen I poured my lifeline, coffee. Double cream, double sugar.

The kids didn't deserve to feel my frustration. This wasn't a good way to kick off a church morning. I breathed in and out. Once, twice.

Eight-year-old Jake ran through the kitchen. "Mom, who was that on the phone?" He took a cold Pop-Tart, pausing to hear my answer before he sprinted back to the couch.

"Just your Aunt Cruella," I whispered. Out loud I said, "Aunt Claudia."

Claudia, the 'mom' in Tom's life, is an over-protective sister who feels she can regularly intrude.

On our third date in high school, Tom drove me to the top of a butte popular with high school couples for stargazing, snuggling and quiet talks. That night, he shared with me it was the six-year anniversary of the death of his parents. I held Tom as he told me the story of how his parents died in a single-car accident. He was eleven, and the only family he had left was his older sister of seven years, Claudia. She raised him through acne, proms, exams, and graduation. After that night at the butte, we both knew we would marry each other one day.

Tom always left early on Sunday mornings. Today he had an eight o'clock open house scheduled before the eleven o'clock church service. These Sunday events added to his success as a real estate agent, earning him the title of top-producer for his company five years in a row, but—

"Once, just once, why couldn't he be home on a Sunday morning?" I asked the casserole dish soaking in cold, oily water from the night before. "Then, he would understand what I go through."

Resting in the sink, the dish ignored me.

"Lord, it's me, Lucy. Forgive me," I whispered, hoping this would make amends for my rotten attitude on a Sunday. Anyway, it was Claudia's fault.

"Adam, Jake, Suzy!" I plunked down three bowls, three spoons, a gallon of milk and a box of cereal. "Breakfast is ready."

"I got my breakfast already," Jake yelled from the couch. He held up his half-eaten Pop-Tart while staring at the television. He took another bite and sat mesmerized by the green ninjas that jumped around the screen.

"Mom, make Suzy stop singing. I can't hear the TV!" Adam yelled.

"She's only six and doesn't understand ninjas." Truth be told, neither did I. "You kids march in here for breakfast right now."

Adam, Suzy, and finally Jake jumped onto the stools, frowning at the cardboard box on the counter.

I tousled Jake's brown hair and gave Suzy a kiss on the forehead as I walked past them. "Sorry about the cold breakfast, guys. Cooperate with me, okay? I'll make you a nice dinner tonight, I promise."

"Okay." They grumbled in unison.

I dashed back to my bedroom to dress. Bent over in the small closet, I flung shoes to the side, one by one, searching for the match to my high heels, which coordinated with my beige dress. Standing up, I pulled at the too tight waist.

Ugh. Mirrors don't lie. I turned sideways, sucked in my tummy and held my breath until it hurt. *How did this happen? All this weight on a five-foot-five body.*

I thought about the photos from the night before, especially the one on the beach that showed my tan, athletic body.

My stomach looked like rising bread dough, complete with stretch marks and indents. I poked my middle. I turned halfway around and hoped the rear view looked better than my profile. My throat tightened. Fat thoughts poured into my mind. I tried to will them away, but all I could think of was how awful I looked. I'd be the frump at church, surrounded by young fashionable women. I was sure every woman at church had married a plastic surgeon. They were all anorexic and proud of it. Pretty and gorgeous, as if they had just stepped off a runway stage. Plus rich and married to prominent doctors, lawyers, and politicians.

Tom and I loved the music and the messages of our church, but I wished our congregation looked like the one I grew up with. Silver hair, walking canes, and plump old ladies.

"Mom," Adam yelled. "Dad's here. We're going to be late." He rushed past my bedroom door. "I have your Bible. You find your purse," he commanded with as much authority as a ten-year old could muster.

"I'm coming." I stole one more glance at myself in the mirror, my pale blue eyes clouded with tears. I lifted my chin, swung my purse strap onto my shoulder and headed out the door. I speed walked to the car.

Tom tapped his fingers on the steering wheel as I slid into the car. His tan business suit with brown pin stripes set off his caramel complexion and brown eyes. Tom had the kids already buckled in and a coffee treat waiting for me.

"Thanks for the coffee, Babe. I appreciate it." I bit my lip to keep from apologizing for being late, skipping the dishes, and well, not looking like I did twelve years ago.

At the modern, stone-front church, Tom maneuvered the SUV into the allotted yellow lines, and I hurriedly applied another layer of powder foundation over the adult acne that dotted my face.

The kids scurried off to the separate children's church wing, while we continued on to the main sanctuary. Greeters welcomed us into the foyer with warm, but staged, smiles that resembled those on mannequins at Macys. With a handshake and a "God bless you," they handed us our morning bulletin.

The earth toned walls soothed and the cushioned pews welcomed us. The drumbeat and rhythmic singing grew louder. The modern hymn was contagious and my lips moved to the words, as I scanned the congregation for a seat.

"Great, Lucy," Tom whispered. "That's just great." He walked beside me with his arm around my waist. "We're late and there aren't any seats left."

"Over there." I pointed to the two empty spots that Julie, my best friend, and her husband Pete saved for us. We scooted into the pew next to them.

"Thanks, Pete." Tom pushed his Bible under the seat in front of him.

The music slowed and the drums softened. Tom leaned over and whispered, "You look nice this morning."

Even after thirteen years of marriage he still made me blush.

The minister, who was in his early thirties, ran up the three steps to the microphone and with a rich, deep baritone voice read the upcoming week's events from the church bulletin.

Julie's favorite perfume, Vera Wang, wafted around me when she whispered in my ear, "See her? Over there, third seat, fourth row?"

"Uh-huh." Never taking my eyes off the bulletin.

"She's Mrs. Oregon."

I looked up and opened my mouth. Julie now had my full attention. "What?"

"She's Mrs. Oregon." Julie's big brown eyes, decorated with too much eye shadow, brightened. "As in a pageant queen."

"You mean 'Miss,' right?" I raised one eyebrow.

"Nope, it's a married woman's pageant."

Mrs. Oregon? Her full face and wide shoulders made her at least appear a few pounds overweight, nothing like the pageant queens on television. She didn't appear flashy. Definitely didn't stand out in the crowd. She wore slacks, a plain solid blue shirt, and little makeup. Her face had a slight remembrance of acne from her teenage years. Her brown hair was pulled back in a ponytail, which accentuated her round face. Boy, I could relate to this woman.

Julie leaned over as I scoped her out. "I heard she lost fifty pounds in ten months."

"Wow." I glanced over my right shoulder, hoping no one heard us gossiping. In church, no less. "She must be... really nice?"

"Shhh." Pete gave us a look.

Julie stifled a laugh.

After what seemed to be the length of an infomercial, the minister finished reviewing the bulletin and began his sermon. I could never concentrate—the sanctuary was brimming with fascinating people. Young couples who seemed to have popped out of the latest *GQ* and *Cosmo* magazines.

In the pew in front of us sat a woman sporting the latest hairstyle and makeup technique, while another woman dressed in fashionable clothes and wore a wedding ring with a diamond the size of a golf ball.

I studied my hands. Dry and chapped. Nails short and chipped. I hid them under my thighs. I should have filed my nails and used clear polish. I'd never noticed so much flashy nail polish in one place. I silently chuckled at my own sarcasm.

The minister ended his sermon and prayed. The four of us filed out of our row to congregate in the lobby, with our other long-time friends, like we did every Sunday.

"I'll meet up with you in a second," I told Julie, nodding my head toward the restroom.

In the stall I wrestled with my too-tight nylons, but stopped when my name was mentioned.

"Poor Lucy. She's really put on the 'L-bees.'"

"It's gotta be killin' her. She used to be so fit."

Ice flowed through my veins and I froze to hear them better.

"That beige dress from a decade ago doesn't help her figure any," the first lady continued.

"I knew her from high-school. She was athletic and cute. She married Tom, the school's football star."

"I wonder what he thinks about her now? I bet—"

The door slowly closed behind them to muffle the last of her statement.

I didn't know whether to be mad or sad. I chose devastated. I couldn't cry. My legs turned to gelatin, I didn't want to leave the bathroom and walk past them. I took my time, washed my hands, and applied lip-gloss before meeting with my friends in the lobby. My stomach curdled and my heart performed a giant ka-bump.

The Gang, as we called ourselves, stood in the usual spot greeting one another with handshakes, slaps on the backs, or hugs. Selena and Colleen chatted about the latest movie. Their husbands talked about yesterday's college football game.

I angled my body perfectly, so if Mrs. Oregon walked by I could capture a closer look at her. I scanned the crowd, but Mrs. Oregon was nowhere to be seen.

"Are you okay, Lucy?" Julie asked. Her voice dropped. "You're so quiet."

"Just fine, thanks." I forced a smile.

"Did you hear about Oprah's latest weight loss program and—?" The pounding of our children's footsteps interrupted Julie.

Suzy skipped over to me, chocolate-brown curls swaying, and pulled on my skirt. Looking down into her smiling face took me back to myself at the age of six. She inherited my facial features, bone structure, and pouty lips, but not the curse of my thick, natural curly strawberry blonde hair. Women told me all of the time they wished they had my hair. I couldn't imagine why. I brushed a strand away from my face.

"Let's go, Mom. I'm hungry." Suzy tugged on my skirt again.

"All right, sweetheart." I knelt, tied her shoe, then smiled up at her. "Gather your brothers and we'll start home."

The warmth of the sun felt good through the car window during the long drive from church. I was quiet, absorbed with thoughts about the bathroom chatter and Mrs. Oregon. She had smashed my image of a beauty pageant winner. I rested my eyes and dreamed of becoming the next Mrs. Oregon. If she did it, maybe I could too.

Tom touched my arm. "What's up, Hon?"

I heard him, but how was I supposed to answer? I wanted to show those ladies in the bathroom, under all this extra skin, I was beautiful. I wanted to be the next Mrs. Oregon.

"Lucy?"

"Sorry. Nothing." I turned my head away.

"Can't put it into words?"

I nodded, and he left me to my mental tug-of-war.

Tom's observations of my mood brought back memories of how terrible my elementary and junior high years were.

Pronunciation, writing words, and sentence structure were obstacles for me and still haunt me today. My classmates pointed and laughed every time I made the dreaded walk of shame to the special speech and Title-1 English class. A girl once mockingly said, "Ask her to say the word *toilet*, she says, 'toll-let.'" Another time a boy yelled, "Have her say the word *feminine*." A burst of laughter followed me when I hurried from the classroom and rushed down the hallway.

The emotional scars lingered, down deep, and sometimes I'd pick at them. To survive in a world built on communication, I learned tricks to disguise my inadequacies. If I entered a pageant, it would rip the scab open.

Tom knew me well and understood why I was a person of few words. I played up my handicap to remain unseen and unheard, whenever I wanted to hide. Tom teased me at times, "Most women I know have the gift of gab."

Tom drove past Claudia's church. A red brick building, which showcased a tall white cross. "Look. There's Claudia's car, still at church." He pointed at the crowded parking lot.

I knew what he thought. He could eat a sandwich and watch four holes of golf on television before Claudia's pastor dismissed the congregation.

"Did she call you again this morning?" Tom laughed.

"Yep." I rolled my blue eyes and returned to daydreaming...me onstage in front of an audience...the lights low, a spotlight dancing on me...speaking eloquently into a microphone about how I would address world peace...cameras snapped and flashed and popped...the crowd clapping and cheering...a crown being placed on my head...roses filling my arms...and my victory walk.

~TWO~
Friends

Hints of autumn appeared everywhere as the month passed. Days shortened. Nights lengthened. Orange, red, and brown leaves spiraled downward landing on mushy soil and dewy grass. The clean smell of October washed the air.

I folded another pair of Tom's underwear, glanced out the window at the bright moon and saw Tom pull in the driveway.

He hummed, *You Are My Sunshine*, as he trotted up the porch steps. His keys jingled to the tune, as he unlocked the front door.

"You're in an extra good mood tonight." I leaned around a mound of clean, unfolded laundry on the sofa to smile at my husband, standing in the doorway.

Tom looked at the pile of clothing and chuckled. He shoved it aside and plopped down. "How did I know I would find you here, folding underwear and watching FOX news?" He reached over the clothes and tucked a lock of my hair behind my ear. "Crochet all day?"

My cheeks grew hot. "I'm sorry, Babe. I feel like all I did today was laundry." I lowered my voice. "And that's not even finished."

I reached into my crochet bag, pulled out the tenth scarf. "I did finish something." I sat straight handing Tom my accomplishment, "The last of the scarves today for the soldiers." I smiled and continued to fold clothes, stacking them in neat piles to put into messy drawers.

He didn't seem to notice the toys scattered on the floor and the unopened piles of mail on the coffee table. *After four years in this house, we still had no dishwasher, no pantry and come to think of it, no maid. What a pipedream.*

Tom found the television remote under a dishtowel and pushed mute. "Honey, pack your things. Next weekend we're going on a three-day vacation with The Gang." A barrel-sized grin spread on his face and his brown eyes sparkled.

"What?" I dropped an undershirt. *Who'd watch the kids? Who would cover his work load at the office?* I opened my mouth to ask about the details that whirled in my mind but closed it as a determined look settled on his face, a look I recognized.

The same look Tom gave me when he announced we were going to Claudia's house for Thanksgiving dinner. The same look that conveyed Jake could not spend the night at little brat Jimmy's house. The look that said there was no changing his mind.

My words stuck in my throat. A dark cloud descended. I disguised my discomfort by searching through the heap of laundry, looking for a missing sock. How could I tell Tom it wouldn't be fun to go away with a bunch of fit women who owned as many bikinis as I did sweatpants, even if the girls were my best friends? My throat tightened, and my heart raced.

"Lucy? You're too quiet. What's up?"

I caught his gaze and hesitated. "I don't want to go." I said, just above a whisper.

"What? Why?"

Searching for the right words, I decided the kids would be the easiest place to start my excuses.

"Who'll take care of the kids?"

"You're kidding, right?" He chuckled, "Claudia will watch the kids and she'll love it. Besides it's only for two and a half days."

A shudder ran through me, imagining Claudia bossing my children, taking note they don't have a set bedtime and that they eat snacks before dinner. "I'd rather my parents watched them."

Tom shrugged. "Fine, I don't care who, as long as we get away." He pointed the remote at the television and clicked through the channels. "Besides, I need a break." He looked back at me. "We need a break."

Old, fat and ugly, I thought. Like a frayed jigsaw piece that no longer fit into "The Gang" puzzle, no matter how hard you pushed.

I swallowed the rest of my excuses knowing Tom would have a rational response to all of them. Like most men, Tom didn't compare his weight or his fatherly duties or housekeeping abilities to other men as women did with one another.

Life seemed much easier for him than for me.

I sighed, knowing I'd lost this round. "I'll confirm the arrangements first thing tomorrow morning." A lead balloon settled in my stomach.

"I can't wait to get away." A smile took up most of Tom's face.

~

Monday early evening I walked to the closet and opened the doors, studying my selection of unglamorous clothes. Where to begin? I lifted one finger in the air, as if a light bulb had come on over my head. *Try on jeans before you throw them into a suitcase.* "I'm a genius." I picked up a pair of acid-washed jeans, fingering the brass button on the fly.

If only all the girls wore sweats, my packing job would be so much easier.

My collection of sweats contained every color of the kaleidoscope. I lived in them. Heck, I would wear them to church if I thought I could get away with it. Maybe I should call my friends and suggest a sweats-only weekend. Nah, that's silly. There is no way Selena and Julie, with their long legs, would go for that idea. Besides, they would see right through my motive. Every so often Tom questioned my attire, but I always gave him the comfort excuse. Actually, it wasn't an excuse.

He'd toss me a sly grin and say, "Don't you ever get bored wearing sweats?"

I'd shoot back. "No, they're comfy."

"But, it's like you're wearing pajamas—every day."

Poor Tom. He probably wanted to know where the cute petite Lucy he'd married had gone. I wondered the same thing, replaying the conversation I overheard in the ladies room at church.

That beige dress from a decade ago doesn't help her figure.

I stood looking into the closet. Did I dare wear sweatpants on vacation? No, I couldn't be the old married lady who'd let herself go, even if I was ten years older and thirty pounds heavier than my twenty-two year old friends. I wanted to make Tom proud, make him happy I was his wife.

One by one, I slid the hangers across the rod, studying each shirt that hung like worn-out rags. I still couldn't decide what to put in the suitcase.

The noise of restless kids grew from the living room. Adam yelled, "Mom, we're hungry."

I tried to ignore him, but soon all three kids hunted me down. I lured them back to the living room with the chance to watch cartoons and eat warm homemade brownies covered with powdered sugar. I positioned paper towels on each of their laps, making them promise they wouldn't spill crumbs on the couch or carpet.

After they were settled, I tiptoed back into my bedroom, even more determined to find a pair of nice jeans. I dug through piles of clothes in the disorganized, overflowing closet and pushed aside a bag destined for the Goodwill.

There they were—under a stack of sweats—my favorite dark denims with fancy, stitched back pockets. I turned over the tag and winced, three sizes smaller than my favorite comfy sweats. I stepped into the jeans and pulled them up as far as mid-thigh. They didn't budge. I grunted and gave one last final yank, but they wouldn't button, let alone zip. I lay on the bed and tried once more in vain.

As I peeled them off, my foot tangled and I tumbled over. I lay on the floor, remembering when I wore a size four. Those days were gone. That picture in the shoebox of Tom and I at the coast seared my mind.

I found another pair of jeans in a larger size, but they were still too small. I tore through the pile again, and tried them on, one by one.

Even my fat jeans were too tight.

In the midst of my misery, I sank to the floor. I'd have to go on vacation in sweats, not because they were comfy, but because they were the only pants that fit. Mortified. I would be walking around a beautiful vacation spot with beautiful people wearing beautiful bikinis. If only I was The Gangs' cook, I could hide in the kitchen of the rented condo.

Right then and there hugging my knees, head down, I vowed to the beauty gods that I would do whatever it took. Mrs. Oregon's trim figure floated into my mind. Once, my own figure had been just as good. Somehow I had to get it back.

The dreaded weekend vacation arrived. We joined The Gang and caravanned four hours to the mountains. The resort featured groomed walking paths and paved bike trails, which wound their way around the outskirts of the golf course and through cedar trees. The five-bedroom condo overlooked hole number nine to be exact, with a man-made pond and two sand traps. I lingered in the kitchen, admiring the view.

In the adjoining living room Pete, Julie's husband, whistled long and low. "Look at that course. It's a beauty." He peered out the picture window. Our husbands all gathered around.

"This is just like the ninth hole at Evergreen Woods, You know, the par-five I eagled." David said.

"That was just dumb luck." Ron performed an air-golf swing.

"Luck, my foot, all skill."

My attention pulled away when Sandra opened the sliding glass door in the kitchen that led to the private cedar deck, where a hot tub sat. "Hopefully it's full of water." She said.

Selena and Julie rushed to help her remove the lid.

"I'm going to slip into my suit." Colleen dashed past me, to the bedroom designated for her and Mark.

I closed the refrigerator and stood holding my diet soda. Now? It wasn't dark enough to climb into the hot tub.

"Don't we want to wait until tonight to hot tub?" I asked Selena and Sandra, who dipped their hands into the water.

"This water feels divine. I'm not waiting." Selena turned on the jets, before leaving the deck to go to her room. Sandra shrugged, turned, and followed.

Left standing alone I said, "But we haven't unpacked our suitcases." I moseyed into the living room. The men still stood looking at the golf course talking about their game. If I entered the golf conversation, hopefully my girlfriends might forget about me. I did not want to join them in the hot tub, but I could not help but watch for the trio to return in their suits.

Colleen, a platinum blonde with jumbo green eyes and jumbo breasts could put Dolly Parton to shame, strutted out wearing a striking yellow bikini. Colleen liked to show off her cleavage, even in church. She was boisterous and light bounced off her porcelain white teeth when she smiled. I wasn't sure which were more fake—her boobs or her smile. She stepped into the bubbling hot tub.

Water splashed when Selena, with her slender long legs, and raven hair, slid down beside Colleen. Selena was a natural beauty, who never wore makeup. Her voice was soft and gentle, and she had the gift of humor.

They giggled like teenagers, as the water lapped around them. Sandra was loud and liberal. All of us liked to gang up on her. We teased her without mercy about doing the opposite of her eco-friendly, recycling ways just to get a reaction from her. Sandra wore expensive, organic clothes and earthy shoes. She was easy to like and she accepted us just the way we were.

Julie, the woman I was closest to, was the athlete in the group, conscious about fitness and her body proved it. Her long, toned legs and short, spiky, blonde hair made her attractive. Along with her sweet smile and generous personality she would do anything for anyone. She joined Selena, Colleen and Sandra in the hot tub.

These were my friends.

Although different from me, our church was the common denominator which joined us together.

"Lucy," Julie yelled, "Hurry up and get your suit on."

From the picture window, I shook my head and held up my soda, pointing at it as if to show I was too busy quenching my thirst to suit up.

"Come on, Lu. Get in." Selena beckoned with her hand.

"The waters great." Sandra added.

"Okay," I mouthed. I set my soda can on the coffee table and scurried to our room, hoping they'd forget about me. Sandra's voice followed me down the hall, "Lucy, hurry up! Get your suit on and join us."

On this cool late afternoon the hot tub did sound divine. I'd have to go to a fat-farm-boot-camp, before I'd let them or anyone else see me in a bathing suit.

I poked my head out of our room and shouted, "I can't find it. I must have left my suit at home. Sorry, guys." I ducked back into the room and pretended to rifle through my suitcase. There wasn't a ghost of a chance I would let anyone see me half-naked.

Almost down the hall, I stopped when Colleen yelled, "Put on your shorts and a tank top then."

I shuddered. "Be right there." I turned back around. No excuses. Now, I had to join them. I thrashed out of my sweats and tossed my T-shirt on the floor. Standing there, I vowed to the diet gods, this time, I'd change. I had to. My self-respect and holding Tom's attention depended on it.

Self-pity turned into anger. Anger turned into determination. I vowed never to be embarrassed to wear a swimsuit again.

No one was going to rescue me from the sand trap I built around myself like the one I saw on hole number nine. Only I could dig myself out.

Mrs. Oregon rescued herself. Why am I even thinking about her? Then, I heard it from somewhere in the far recesses of my mind. *Enter a beauty pageant.* I didn't know a thing about entering a pageant. I wasn't the pageant type. All that glitzy jewelry, fancy gowns, and bright red lipstick—yuck. Besides, with this body, I wouldn't make it past the first round.

No, I could change. I had to change. I gritted my teeth, as I slid my tank top on over my head.

Do it! Don't tell anyone, not even Tom, my parents, or The Gang…and especially, not Claudia.

A slow grin came over my face.

At this stage of the game, I didn't need any naysayers. My mind was set. I would enter a pageant. No one could talk me out of it. As soon as this mini-vacation ended, I would research pageants. I didn't have a clue where to begin or what I was getting into. I just knew I had to try.

With my decision made, I stole six Oreos and a tall glass of milk on my way through the kitchen to face the hot tub. Then, I started the mental clock. Only twenty-nine and a half hours to go until Operation Pageant began.

~THREE~
Overload

Shh, don't wake the kids." I reminded Tom while he opened the front door, our hands full of luggage. The living room floor looked bigger than ever. No toys, books or broken crayons scattered around. My clean laundry had disappeared from the end of the couch, replaced by Grandma and Grandpa relaxing in front of the television.

"We're home," I sang, keeping my voice low. I collapsed on the couch hugging several magazines I had buried myself in, from cover to cover, while on vacation.

"Did the kids wear you out?" Tom dropped his suitcase by the front door. "Everyone still alive?" He winked at my mother.

"Yep." My dad cleared his throat, trying with not much success, to sound wide-awake. "We're just coming up for air." He took his time pushing himself up from the couch.

"Thanks, Mom and Dad. I hope they behaved." I said.

"Of course. They're little angels." Grandma gave a playful smile.

Grandpa looked up toward heaven. "I just finished polishing their halos."

Suzy ducked around the corner from the kitchen with a sly grin. I blew her a kiss, before she dashed back to bed.

"Claudia dropped by to see if we needed any help," Mom said.

My body stiffened at the mention of her name.

"That was nice of her." Tom sat on the arm of the couch.

"You told her no, right? I mean, you didn't need help or anything?" I shrugged like it didn't bother me that she had stopped in to snoop on my motherly duties. "The house looks great, Mom. Did you pick things up *before* Claudia came or after?" I stressed 'before' a little too loudly. "I mean, she didn't see the mess I left you, did she?"

"No, Honey. Your father and I had already picked up the toys and cleaned the kitchen before she popped in." She gave me an understanding smile.

I held back a high five and mouthed, "Thanks."

We visited awhile with Mom and Dad before they gathered their belongings, put on their jackets, and hugged us good-bye.

Once the front door closed behind them I fired at Tom. "Why would Claudia stop by? Did she think my parents didn't have everything under control?"

Tom's eyes narrowed and he scratched his head. "Lucy, you should be thankful she stopped by. She missed her work meeting to stop in and check on the kids."

"Work meeting? How do you know that?"

He paused, a bit too long, and it hit me. "Wait, you called her and asked her to come and check on my parents, didn't you?" I knew his answer before he said anything.

"Now, Lucy." He shook his head. "It's not like that." He put his arm around me.

I pulled away. "No? So, you had her check on the kids, then? Is that it?" I waved my arms.

"Before you get mad, hear me out."

"Get mad? I'm already mad. I can't believe you did that Tom." I picked up a suitcase. "Good thing Mom had the house picked up, or I would have to hear Claudia's zingers on my lack of housekeeping skills for the next six months." I stormed to our bedroom and tossed the suitcase on the floor amongst all the other clutter.

"Don't be ridiculous, Lucy." Tom's words followed me. "You're paranoid." He turned on the evening news.

I slammed the door and leaned my back against it, sniffling to fight back tears. Tom never understood how inadequate his sister makes me feel. She'd let me know too many times how I wasn't good enough for her baby brother. I sniffled again, but this time I couldn't stop the tears.

I glanced at the suitcase on the floor. I'd deal with that rectangle canvas box tomorrow, or the day after that. Hopefully I wouldn't stub my toe on it, during a middle-of-the night bathroom run. I sank into our waterbed, closed my heavy eyelids and enjoyed the silence. Soon I drifted off to sleep, still wearing my sweats.

~

My alarm went off at 7:30 a.m. the next morning, determined to set Operation Pageant into motion as soon as Tom left for work. If anyone told me yesterday I'd compete for the title of Mrs. Oregon in my thirties, with three children and sprouting gray hair, I would've told them they were as crazy as clowns with big, red noses squishing into little, painted cars.

I jumped out of bed, hopped over the suitcase and rushed to the kitchen to fix oatmeal and toast for Tom and the kids.

After the front door clicked shut behind them, I poured myself another cup of coffee and sat down at our dinosaur of a computer. The monster was slow. I sipped my coffee and waited for the internet connection. Dust hopped in the sunrays for a few seconds, before it settled on the computer screen. I blew the cookie crumbs out of the keyboard and stacked the loose papers scattered around the desk. *Someday, I would get organized.*

The search engine field appeared, I typed *pageants*, hit enter and waited. Information, bit by bit, rolled up on my screen for the Junior Miss pageants, Miss Teen pageants, pre-teen pageants, and every other age, but no data appeared for married women pageants.

After what seemed like hours of searching and getting lost in cyberspace, I narrowed my search by typing *Mrs. Pageants*. A website for a married women's pageant in Oregon scrolled onto my screen.

That was it? A molecule of information?

I clicked on a tab, which redirected me to pageant pictures. I studied each contestant. Examined their hair, their clothes and guessed their ages. They all wore big smiles with sparkling teeth. Another tab read, *Venue and Ticket Information*.

Then on the right side of the screen, a tab on how to enter the pageant. I whipped the mouse pointer onto it and clicked. The page that opened was brief. All I could do was follow the instructions, which told me to call for more information. Now, to find the phone. I located it under a pile of papers on the desk. My knees threatened to fold, so I sat down and dialed the number. While it rang, I bounced back up again and paced, heart beating fast.

Stay calm. Sound confident. Do not fumble for words. Do not hang up.

"Mrs. Oregon headquarters. May I help you?"

I held the phone tight, white knuckled, resting my forehead against the doorjamb to calm myself. "Um, yes, I visited your pageant website and read where I needed to call this number for information. Is that correct?"

"Yes, that's right." Paper shuffled in the background. "What is your mailing address? I'll send you out a packet." *That was all? Easy.*

After the formalities I thanked her and said a polite good-bye. I deleted the website history from the computer.

First step of Operation Pageant completed.

I wasn't ready for Tom, family or friends to find out. I wanted to wait until I was sucked down deep into my plan, like quicksand, where escaping was difficult or impossible, before I sprang the news.

$\sim$

After the phone call to headquarters, my afternoon routine changed. Now, each day, I'd walk through the house with a purpose. I poked my head into each room and made a mental note as to where and what the kids were doing, before I rushed the two hundred yards down the driveway to the mailbox. I didn't want them to see I was eager for something to arrive and begin to ask questions.

Please be here today. I wanted to see an envelope with the return address of Mrs. Oregon headquarters.

Adam noticed. "Mom, how come you keep rushing to the mailbox every day?" Caught. Typical of Adam, he was so observant. A trait he inherited from his father.

"Oh, I do?" I widened my eyes, trying to look surprised. It was imperative the kids not find out about Operation Pageant. If they knew, then their Aunt Claudia would know. If Claudia knew…the whole community would know and someone might try to talk me out of entering.

The weeks of fall disappeared and still no envelope arrived from the pageant. Finally one cold day in the middle of November, I opened the mailbox and looked in. It was here, a large white envelope with the Mrs. Oregon logo in purple stamped on the front. I sprinted back to the house, made sure I was alone, found my cute pink reading eyeglasses and tore into the envelope. I plucked out a mere two sheets of paper. It was like opening a pretty wrapped box with nothing inside but a pair of white socks.

The letter simply stated: *Thank you for your interest in the preliminary to the Mrs. Oregon pageant. We are searching for a contestant from your city, who, if she qualifies will receive an official title and banner. We will accept applicants from your city for approximately one month, after which time, a representative will be chosen and notified, and will hold her title for one year.*

Another month's wait! I wondered how many other married women from my area would apply.

Please fill out the form at the bottom of this page, enclose the application fee (non-refundable). Include a recent photograph of yourself and mail both to headquarters.

Oh brother, a photo. I don't think I even have one without a kid in it.

After we receive your entry fee and the completed application a committee will determine if you are selected to represent your town or city. If so, you will receive a banner with your local area's name.

That was it? That was all it said? It didn't tell me much except there were other applicants. But nothing could stop me from writing a check for the entry fee. My pen hovered over the register. Tom would see the entry and question me. I considered leaving it out. Pretend I forgot to fill in the register. I couldn't believe I thought about hiding this from Tom.

The sun had set an hour ago and Tom would be home soon. I had no choice. It was time. Time to tell him about the pageant. But how? I could drop it lightly on him like morning dew and act like it was no big deal. Or I could go at it like a tornado and throw him into a spin.

After thirteen years of marriage I knew how to tell him. Tom was a practical man and would want me to be honest and get to the point. But…a pageant? I had no idea how he would react. This wasn't the usual, "Hey Babe, can I have a girls' night out with Julie, Selena, Colleen and Sandra?" This was a pageant. And Tom hated the unknown, hated change and hated undue attention on the family. He would balk at me entering a pageant and this wasn't cheap. Cost would be an issue too.

I drummed my fingertips on the windowsill, watching for his car, rehearsing various ways to tell him.

Casual…"Hon, I'm gonna enter a pageant."

Serious…"Tom, sit down. I have something important to tell you."

Tom turned into the driveway and my heartbeat quickened. Before he reached the top of the steps, I swung the door open, threw my arms around his neck and planted a big kiss on his lips. "Guess what I did today?"

"Emptied our suitcase?" Tom kissed me back on the forehead.

"Very funny, Tom. I emptied that last week." I bit my lower lip. "I researched pageants on the Internet a few weeks ago and sent for this information." I waved the paperwork. "I'm going to compete in a pageant and I sent my application fee in today." My words spilled out fast.

"Whoa, slow down, Lucy. Let me sit for this." Tom looked away, pulled off his coat and hung it in the entry closet. "Did you say a pageant? Don't you have to be twenty-something, six-feet tall and *not* married to enter a pageant?"

"That's what I thought too." I cleared my throat. "There is actually a pageant for married women."

There was a long pause. The cogs and wheels had to be turning in Tom's head.

"Why didn't you tell me you were researching pageants?" Tom raised an eyebrow. "Why are you telling me now after you already signed up?" He looked down.

I watched him study the carpet, deep in thought. I didn't know what to say. I hadn't meant to hurt him. I didn't know how to explain something to him that I didn't fully understand.

Tom crossed through the living room to the dining room table and sat.

I followed him. My mind raced with what to say next. The chill of the awkward silence worried me. I cleared the dirty plates from the kids' lunch and handed him copies of the pageant paperwork. I sucked on the end of my glasses and watched his eyes dart back and forth as he studied the papers.

Tom broke the silence. "Please tell me this is just a phase, right Lucy?" He dropped the papers to the table.

"A phase? I'm not a child. I'm your wife."

He let out a nervous laugh before his forehead creased with concern. "You're not really going to follow through with a pageant, are you?"

I squared my shoulders. "Yes, I want to."

The tension grew thick and the silence long while Tom scoured the Mrs. Oregon letter again, probably looking for a reason why I didn't fit the criteria.

Tom dropped his head in his hands, which I misinterpreted as waving the white flag. "How much is this pageant going to cost me?"

"I don't know." I shrugged, twirling my glasses in my hand.

"You do to know." He raised his head. His face held no expression. "How much?"

"I don't know. I guess we'll find out as we go." I didn't want to talk about the cost. "It can't be that much." I tried to sound convincing.

"Lucy, I guess I don't understand why you would want to bring all this attention to yourself."

I looked at him, stupefied. "You think I'm going to embarrass you?"

Tom stood and closed the kitchen blinds. I stood and waited for an answer.

I lowered my voice. "Is it because I'm overweight?"

"No. Gosh, no! Lucy—"

"I want to do this, Tom. I need to do this. For me." My voice quivered. "You don't understand. I've lost my confidence, my self-esteem and my identity."

I talked fast, not letting him speak. "I'm feeling everything drift away as I get older. I am thirty-two years old, and other than raising kids, what have I accomplished?" That had to sting. I regretted my words the minute they flew out of my mouth.

"Lucy, I think it's a waste of money. We don't have it right now to spend on a silly pageant."

I sat at the table and placed my forehead in the crease of my elbow, closed my eyes and felt my pageant momentum fade away. He was right, I wasn't Mrs. Oregon material. I'm a mom and wife first, plus I gained weight, lost touch with the latest fashion and makeup trends. *Accept it, Lucy.*

I opened my eyes. The breadcrumbs on the table glared at me as if to say, you're getting fat. *You're getting fat, didn't you hear us?* I pushed myself away from the table and the crumbs.

I pulled the gallon of chocolate chip mint ice cream from the freezer.

"What are you doing?' Tom asked.

I didn't answer him and scooped three huge mounds of ice cream into a bowl. "Want some?"

Tom looked at me, sadness written across his face.

I jabbed at the ice cream with my spoon. The longer I jabbed the more I tightened my jaw to prevent tears from escaping.

Tom took a step closer and gently took the bowl away from me and set it on the counter. He lifted my chin with his hand. His brown eyes looked straight into mine. "I asked you, 'What are you doing?' Because, the future Mrs. Oregon I know wouldn't be eating ice cream right now. Would she?"

"Really? I can enter?" I folded my arms around his waist.

"Really. "His body relaxed when I hugged him.

"Thank you. Thank you."

"If I have to sell a kidney, I will."

A giggle slipped through my tears. The tears of a dream saved. "Hold on for the ride."

"Just don't lose us, Lucy, in another one of your crazy adventures, okay?" Tom's voice was soft. He pulled me tighter, kissed my neck and held me.

A memory bell rang in my mind. A few years back I begged Tom to buy an old decrepit house for us to fix up. I thought it was a perfect idea at the time, him being a real estate agent. He knew we couldn't afford a rental and he tried to convince me it was not a logical idea, but I was determined.

I envisioned the two of us working late into the night with candles surrounding us on the bare floor as we painted the walls, listening to our favorite CD. Shopping for carpet together, working on a sunny day landscaping and being the proud owners of a second home.

Instead, we came to verbal blows about every renovation decision and how much to spend on repairs. We never found a renter. Finally, after six months of that venture, Tom saved the day. He sold the house before we lost it to the bank.

"I won't. I promise." I pulled away and handed him my spoon. "Here, you eat it."

Tom opened his mouth and chuckled before slurping the ice cream off the spoon.

I wiped the counter top, did a hop and let out a squeal. "I'm gonna call Mom."

"Great, then you can call Claudia."

I gave him a funny look. "Why would I call her? I want people to support me and I'm pretty sure she's not going to like this idea."

"Of course she will."

"Hmmm, maybe. But, I'm going to call Mom first."

Now, to find the phone.

~FOUR~
Special

If nothing had interrupted her routine, Mom would be finishing the final cleaning touches on her perfect 4,500 square foot home.

Tom and I didn't understand why Mom and Dad needed such a large home for the two of them. When we visited we felt like we were stepping into the pages of a *Better Homes & Gardens* magazine. We were always nervous about bringing the kids to their lovely home.

The phone rang twice. "Hello-o-o."

"Hi, Mom."

"Hi. How are you and my beautiful grandkids?"

I blurted, "Mom. Guess what I did?" I glanced at my paperwork.

"No telling, knowing you."

"Guess, Mom. It'll be fun."

"Alright, but you know I hate the guessing game." Mom paused. "You joined a gym."

Ouch, that stung! Now, I hate the guessing game.

"Never mind, I'll just tell you what I did. I entered the Mrs. Oregon Pageant."

After a long pause Mom said, "A pageant? What kind of pageant?"

"A beauty pageant for married women." I didn't dare move until she responded. I pictured my mom on the phone, washing the last dish in the sink or rearranging fresh flowers in the crystal vase on her perfectly clean marble countertop.

"What does Tom think of this idea?"

Of course, she thought of Tom first.

"He's fine with it." I shrugged like it was an everyday occurrence for the Rupp family.

"Really? What did Claudia say?"

"Mom, you know you were my first phone call. Why do I need to inform Claudia?"

Why does everyone care what she thinks?

"Hmmm, okay." Mom sounded careful with her words. "Tell me more."

Her espresso machine hummed in the background steaming milk. I knew she was settling in for a long conversation. I imagined her moving to her plush cream-colored leather sofa with her coffee, ready to listen to my big dream. I wanted her to catch my excitement like a television drama. I spent the next ten minutes telling her what little I knew about the pageant, starting with the church sighting of Mrs. Oregon. Mom's interest seemed to increase with every detail.

"Let me get my daily planner, so we can schedule a trip to go shop for your pageant clothes." She was the only person I knew who organized shopping sprees.

I wish I were as organized.

Neither of us knew much about pageants, other than what we saw on television. It wasn't long before I soon learned that my idea, her idea, and the pageant system's idea about wardrobe were three different ideas.

Now I needed to call Claudia. If she was the last to know she might be upset. Besides it would make Tom happy. It was late but I knew she would still be awake.

I picked up the phone to dial, when the telephone rang.

"Hello."

"Hi, Lucy."

"I just picked up the phone to call you. How weird." I wondered why she was calling me, but knew I would soon find out.

"I wanted to tell you I took your ironing basket home with me the other night when I checked in on my nephews and niece. Thought you should know, in case Tom needed a business shirt. I'll bring the clothes by in the morning."

She what? I dashed to the coat closet where I kept my basket. Sure enough, gone.

I scrunched my face and slapped my forehead. "Uh, okay. Thank you. I was going to iron tomorrow." I crossed my fingers and swung my hand behind my back.

"You're welcome. See you tomorrow."

"Good night." I put the phone down, forgetting on purpose to tell her about the pageant.

"Who was that?" Tom called from the living room.

"Cruella." I joined Tom on the sofa.

"What did she want?"

"To tell me I'm no Martha Stewart and she had to iron your business shirts, because I didn't do them. She thinks I'm a horrible wife and you know it."

"Lu, you know that's not what she thinks. She just wants to help." He massaged the back of my neck.

"So, did you tell her about the pageant?"

"Not yet. I will tomorrow when she brings your shirts on a silver platter." I put a couch pillow on Tom's lap and laid my head on it.

He brushed my bangs back and ran his fingers through my hair while we watched 20/20.

Tomorrow would be soon enough to tell Claudia about my latest plan.

❧

The next morning, pouring myself a cup of coffee, the front door creaked.

"Hel-loo." Claudia floated in, her arms full with the ironing basket.

She never knocks.

"Good morning," I said. "Did you pass Tom coming in the house? He just left for work." I took a sip of my coffee.

"Yes. He said you had some great news to tell me."

"He did?" I looked down. I didn't know if I should be mad at him because I had to tell Claudia now, or be happy he prepared the way for a bumpy conversation. "It's no big deal, really. I…uh…entered a beauty pageant."

Claudia froze and scrutinized me. Rarely did she look puzzled, but this time, I knew I surprised her. "A beauty pageant? Don't you have to be single?"

Does everybody think that?

"This is a pageant for married women."

"Why would you want to put yourself out there for everyone to judge you? Don't you have to wear a swimsuit? Aren't pageants expensive and time consuming?"

"Yes, yes, and yes to all of the above. Actually, it's not going to be that expensive or time consuming." *Was I trying to convince Claudia or myself?* "Do you want some coffee?" I turned to walk back into the kitchen.

"Why a pageant?"

I didn't feel like explaining myself to Tom's older sister, of all people. "I thought I needed to do something for myself for a change. I'm always trying to please everyone else, so I decided this time I'm going to do something for me." I held eye contact with her, until she looked away first. "Claudia, to be honest, I'm entering because I need something to motivate me to take care of myself. Look at me. I'm only thirty-two, overweight, out of style and I have no…" I couldn't finish my statement. I couldn't come out and say the truth…*I'm just boring.*

With each passing day, my hopes of being selected for the Mrs. Oregon Pageant grew dimmer. Winter was now in the air. Dark clouds struggled to drop snowflakes.

Tom entered the kitchen, a stack of mail under one arm, a briefcase in the other. An official looking manila envelope peeked out. My heart pounded. "Is that what I think it is?"

Tom nodded with a playful grin, holding it high above his head as I lunged for it. "You don't really want to see it, do you?"

"Tom!" I couldn't believe he would tease me at a time like this.

"It's here, Lucy." He lowered his hand and gave it to me. "I know you can't wait to open it."

I grabbed the envelope before he could yank it away again and playfully punched him in the arm. The firmness of his bicep spun me back to our high school days.

Tom, an all-star football player at Springfield High, would stride down the school hallway with his buddies, laughing and rough housing. On game days he wore his letterman's jacket with a pigskin tucked under his arm and I wore my cheerleading outfit. Kids referred to us as Ken and Barbie. The memory vanished, when Tom said, "Open it."

"Here goes." I ripped into the envelope. The first thing my fingers found was a satin banner. As I pulled out the slippery fabric, a piece of paper floated to the ground.

Tom snatched it before it touched down and whisked it behind his back.

"Give it to me." I stomped my foot childlike then gave a seductive smile. "Pleeease."

"Not until you say the three magic words." Tom smiled as his words again brought back memories of our high school dating days when he stole my homework before I turned it in to the teacher.

"Come on, Tom. Give it to me." I stuck out my bottom lip in a mock pout and crossed my arms.

"Not until you say those three words." He repeated, holding the paper above his head.

I jumped for it, but of course, I couldn't reach the eight-foot dangling carrot.

He read out loud. "Dear Lucy," he paused for dramatic effect, glanced at me from the corner of his eye and lowered his voice to boom like a trombone. "I am sorry to inform you that you were not accepted to compete in the Mrs. Oregon Pageant." He paused again.

"Oh, Tom, it doesn't say that! Stop teasing," I tightened my ponytail. "I know that's not true or I wouldn't be holding this satin ribbon thing. Now give me the letter. I can't wait any longer."

"Three words, Lu, and it's all yours." Tom said in a manly yet singsong tone of voice, raising the paper even higher.

"All right, if I must." I huffed. "You're—the—best," I said without conviction.

"Say it again but this time, mean it." Tom stepped closer and kissed me on my nose.

"You're. The. Best." My voice was soft and sincere.

"Now that wasn't so hard, was it?" Tom held a smug grin. He handed me the crinkled letter, peeking over my shoulder, kissing my neck.

I pretended to clear my throat and read out loud. *"Dear Lucy, Congratulations! Our judges have reviewed the applications from your area and have chosen you as Mrs. Springfield, Oregon."*

I pushed my eyeglasses up and continued to read.

"Once you accept this title, you qualify to compete in the Mrs. Oregon Pageant. Please fill in the enclosed forms and return them immediately, along with a check for the first installment, payable to the Mrs. Oregon headquarters."

I squealed then jumped up and down around the kitchen. I glanced at Tom leaning against the kitchen counter with his arms folded while I performed my victory dance. He stared over my head, pretending not to watch my joyful antics.

I shrugged it off. Of course, he was happy for me. I took several deep breaths, planted my butt in the dining room chair and continued to read aloud. *"Both you and your husband need to sign the enclosed contestant contract."*

Tom dropped a kiss on my cheek. "I'm going to leave you to it."

"Where are you going? There's more."

"To watch a real victory dance. Football is on."

I fastened my banner across my chest that stated *'Mrs. Springfield'*, swiped the camera off the counter and sashayed into the living room dangling it in front of him. "Take a picture of me holding my congratulatory letter and wearing my banner."

He snapped a few shots. "You should start a Facebook page it would be a good way to promote yourself."

I could always count on Tom to come up with good ideas. I pursed my lips and let out a mwah sound, "You're right. This pageant is going to be so much fun." I swung my hips in an exaggerated model's walk back into the kitchen and sat at the dining table to read more of the guidelines.

Along with my banner and congratulatory letter the packet included information about venue, the different phases of competition, scoring procedure, ad pages, bio questionnaire for the judges, how to sell tickets, appearances, deadlines and payments and how to choose a platform.

I stared at the wall, pondering. A platform. At least that would be easy—speech therapy for children.

Inside the envelope was a coupon for one free magazine issue of *Pageantry*. I loved to read. I loved new challenges. And I loved coupons.

Without hesitation, I filled out the coupon for the free magazine and I didn't stop there. I checked the box for a whole year's subscription.

Popping out of my chair, I spun around and around in the kitchen.

Finally, I would be someone special.

Finally, I would accomplish a huge feat.

And finally, people would have to acknowledge me. I was entering the big-time.

~FIVE~
Extraordinary

My happiness burst a few days later when I learned any married woman who paid an entry fee would be eligible to compete. Pageant headquarters would find a city or county for a woman to represent, regardless of where she lived.

Contestants did not have to compete with any other woman for a city or county title. I wasn't special after all, but I didn't care. I wore my title, Mrs. Springfield, like a peacock showing off his beautiful feathers.

Eventually, I realized, it took someone special to walk out on stage and let a panel of judges and an audience critique her. It took someone with confidence to talk and walk in front of a crowd. I had to believe in myself, work hard and build self-esteem. I wanted to become someone extraordinary.

~

A high-pitched tone came from my alarm clock, sending shock waves through my sleeping body.

"Is that your alarm clock, this early?" Tom rolled over and smashed his pillow over his head.

I bounced out of bed. "I'm starting my exercise regimen today." I went to the closet and rummaged through the stacks of clothes. "Shouldn't be too hard to find a pair of sweats."

"You're what?" The pillow muffled his voice.

"I'm dreading having to wear a swimsuit in front of an audience," I groaned. "I'm going for an easy jog, lift some weights and then stretch. I need to look my best wearing a swimsuit on stage. It's worth twenty-five percent of the overall score." I unraveled the earphone wire to my iPod.

"I should have known this had something to do with pageants." Tom turned over and gave his pillow a good smack.

"I need to lose thirty pounds, Honey. You'll be happy once I do." I raised one eyebrow. "I can't afford to wait until the last minute before the pageant to begin a diet program. I have to start now. I have to be committed and dedicated." My motivational speech was more for my benefit than to convince him. He merely groaned again and settled back to sleep for another hour.

Stepping outside I ignored the crisp air on my face while I searched for an upbeat song on my iPod. Once I found a tune, I put one foot in front of the other slowly.

Reeeeally slow. I shook my head. I used to run half marathons for goodness sake.

Ten minutes into my jog, my legs were heavy and my arms were weak, but nothing was going to discourage me from my goal. I visualized my physique shrinking and my confidence and self-esteem building. I had one goal—to win the pageant. It ran continuously through my mind refusing to let me off the hook, even for a moment. Though I had to admit the thought of crawling back into my warm bed, maybe with a few bon-bons, did cross my mind.

Exhausted and soaked in sweat, I arrived back home. I knew what I needed to do. Move jogging to the number one spot on my priority list. I took a quick shower, applied light makeup and gathered my hair in a ponytail to prepare for my big pageant shopping trip with Mom. I was eager to start. I picked another pair of sweats. After all, they would be the most comfortable and easiest to slip in and out of in the dressing rooms.

After the kids loaded onto the school bus, I drove the twenty miles to pick up Mom. We zipped through an espresso stand and ordered my mocha and Mom's black coffee, then headed to the mall.

During the drive, I chatted non-stop, fueled by the coffee beans and exercise buzz. "I can't wait, Mom. This pageant is going to be so much fun. Do you think I have a chance to win?"

"Of course, Honey. I think the judges will love you like we do." Mom thumbed through the pageant magazine I had left on her seat.

"You *have* to say that. You're my mom."

"This article recommends hiring a pageant coach. Have you considered the idea?"

"A pageant coach?" This sub-culture was more complex than I thought. "I didn't know there was such a person. I'll research it the moment I get home and settled."

I continued to talk, as Mom listened to my dreams. All of my life, she never once discouraged me, even the time in my senior year of high school when I joined the drama club and auditioned for a school play. Back then, I was full of self-assurance, confidence and a belief I could do anything. She was there to comfort me when I only made it as far as a stand-in for *Annie Get Your Gun*.

The mall greeted us with dazzling lights, elevators, escalators and the noise of a hundred voices. The smell of cinnamon rolls enticed us. Mom and I looked at each other and, with a head-nod, agreed to walk fast, leaving the temptation behind. Once we were far enough from the sweet, cinnamon aroma she pulled out a list. "You'll need an interview outfit."

"You made a list? Mooom" She was crazy about lists. I rolled my eyes at the realization I didn't think to write a list. "There's JC Penny. Let's start there."

Inside the bright store I piled Mom's arms full of polyester suits of every color before entering the largest dressing room with a tri-fold mirror.

"Is this one too tight?" I opened the jacket to see if my tummy bulge showed.

"No, but it sure is orangey." She frowned.

Mom and I were wearing a pathway in the carpet from the racks of polyester suits to the dressing room. When finally I found one we both agreed on, black with a little white collar and four half dollar size white buttons down the front. It fit perfectly.

Standing in line at the cash register, I ignored the price tag and fumbled for my credit card. I told myself I deserved it.

"What's next?" I swung the bag in rhythm with my steps. Secretly, I was glad Mom had thought to make the list.

"Evening gown."

We dodged in and out of several stores. "I'm getting worried, Mom. No stores carry evening gowns."

Eventually we found a store that sold prom dresses. A sophisticated saleslady, with each silver hair sprayed in place, darted through the narrow path around the racks of clothes and asked Mom what she was looking for.

"My daughter is looking for an evening gown for a beauty pageant."

The sales lady turned and studied my figure. I took a step behind Mom.

She gave me a warm smile. "Let's begin."

The three of us gathered dresses. Lots of dresses. After trying on the fourteenth formal dress, weary and hair full of static, I stepped out of the changing room.

Mom clapped her hands and smiled. "Beautiful."

"I think so, too." I spun around with a huge smile. "I feel elegant."

"Actually, I prefer the blue gown," Ms. I-know-my-stuff saleslady said. Mom and I looked at each other. Silence. She wasn't successful in convincing me to change my mind. I had found a dress both Mom and I agreed was beautiful.

The sleek, black, fitted, velour floor-length gown slenderized my body. A white chiffon scarf loosely wrapped from the front neckline and flowed down the back in a train, like a moonbeam against a black sky.

At the counter, I handed my credit card to the clerk in slow motion, trying not to cringe at the price. I justified this cha-ching by knowing the black and white colors matched my interview suit.

"Next is a swimsuit." Mom said, leaving the store.

"Let's pass on that one," I sighed.

"Why? I thought with your interview suit being black and white and your evening gown black and white, you should buy a black and white swimsuit. That way you will have a color theme throughout the entire pageant."

"That's a great idea. I like it. But I don't want to buy a suit today. I need to lose more weight." Besides my feet hurt, the garment bags were heavy, my stomach growled and my credit card was maxed out. I wanted shopping to be done.

After we chose a salad for our dinner, I dropped Mom off at her home. I drove into our driveway a flash of movement in the front window captured my attention. Drawing closer, Tom paced back and forth with the telephone to his ear, this couldn't be good. He waved to me through the window and ended the phone call, rushed down the steps and helped me gather my purchases from the trunk of the car.

"There you are. I just called your mom." He slammed the trunk. "Whoa, this is heavy. What is it?" he asked, as he walked up the front steps.

"It's my evening gown. I can't wait to put it on and show you." I followed behind him.

"And I can't wait to see it." Tom handed off my garment bag as I passed through the living room to the bedroom to prepare for an exclusive fashion show. He sat on the couch remote in hand while I quickly changed.

"Ready or not, here I come." I kicked one leg around the corner.

Tom started to sing, "Da daaa da daa," from the old-fashioned stripper song.

"Oh Tom, stop that." I chuckled. "Don't make me laugh." Taking in a deep breath I straightened my shoulders. One step at a time I passed in front of the television, across the living room, shook my booty, pivoted and strutted back in front of him. "It's a little tight, but I'm going to lose weight and it'll fit perfectly."

Tom humored me and sat through my twirling and prancing in high heels that pinched my toes.

"Looks like you need some practice balancing on those shoes."

"Am I wobbling?"

"Don't worry. You'll get it." He encouraged. "That evening gown is stunning. Tom raised an eyebrow. "How much did it cost?"

"You would spoil the moment, wouldn't you?" I put my hand on my hip, turned and left the room to change.

"When will you ever wear it again?" Tom's voice followed me.

I returned to the living room wearing sweatpants and a T-shirt. I dreaded telling Tom about my plan to find a coach. I had to tell him and not wait any longer. Unable to think of a clever way to announce it, I blurted, "Mom suggested I find a pageant coach." I stood in front of Tom, hands on hips, blocking his view of the TV.

"A pageant coach? Like pageants are a sport? Ha."

"I called a modeling school to see if they knew of a coach, and they did," I said with a can-you-believe-it tone.

"Of course they did."

"Her name is Courtney. I made an appointment for tomorrow."

"You already made the appointment?"

"That's why I called."

"How much does she cost?"

"I'm sure she is affordable besides if I'm going to enter a pageant I need to do things right."

"And you think hiring a coach is doing things right? It's all perspective."

"Perspective, I don't have yet."

"Lucy, I wish you would talk to me first about these things, before you just jump in." He shook his head with a look of disgust.

I hated the tone in his voice.

"More money." He bent around me and turned the volume up. The conversation was over and it was fine by me.

I went to bed early to avoid more confrontation. Tom stayed up later than usual. I heard the television tuned in to the familiar sounds of sports reruns.

~

The following morning, I picked Mom up and drove to the address Courtney gave me. We arrived at her beautifully landscaped two-story home at 112 Daffodil Lane. I took a deep breath. "A pageant coach was a great idea, Mom." I bounced in my seat with excitement about what I would learn today. I parked the SUV in the driveway and lingered. I looked at Mom, "Am I ready for this?"

Mom gathered her notebook and pen. "Yes, you are."

Standing on the landing, I rang Courtney's doorbell and rocked back and forth on my heels staring at the pattern of cracks in the cement. I stopped my nervous rocking and put my ear against the Maplewood door.

"Do you hear anything?" A twinge of nervousness cracked in Mom's voice.

"Shhh, someone's coming." I snapped to attention before the door swung open.

Courtney's gentle eyes accompanied her friendly smile. She was tall, lean and gorgeous. "Hello. You must be Lucy." Everything about Courtney was straight. Straight teeth, straight hair, straight posture and she looked me straight in the eye.

"Yes, and this is my mom, Lucinda."

Everything Courtney wore matched perfectly in a cream-colored palette. Her belt and accessories were the perfect shade of cream. Her long brown hair was a beautiful contrast to her off-white blouse. "Welcome, please come in."

We stepped onto the glossy, white marble floor. Her house smelled fresh with a hint of vanilla. Sunshine beamed through the skylight and showcased an oversized bouquet of white roses sitting on a side table to the left. On the right, poster size, portraits of Courtney hung on the wall. I paused to study them. In all of Courtney's photos her complexion was perfect and her makeup held a hint of tan. Glamorous.

Mom and I followed Courtney into her living room. More pictures were placed in fancy, expensive picture frames, nothing cutesy, all displayed in perfect order. Some included her husband and others highlighted a fancy groomed Bichon Frisé.

"You're new to the pageant world, Lucy?" Courtney stepped closer and touched my shoulder.

"Uh-huh."

"Not 'uh-huh.' You must always say 'yes.' That is lesson number one." Courtney laughed with a soft trill. "Welcome to becoming a new person. No matter, win or lose, you will never be the same after a pageant."

Never be the same that sounded good to me.

"Sit, sit, let me get to know you before we start to work." Courtney sat and crossed her ankles in a true queen like fashion on the stiff, mocha colored leather couch. Her Bichon Frisé, wearing a narrow, pink collar with jewels and a tiny bell, skipped up onto her lap.

"What's your doggie's name?" I was thankful for something in the room to lighten the tension I placed on myself.

"Tiara."

To calm myself I reached out to pet her dog.

Tiara jumped down from Courtney's lap and ran out the doggie door to the backyard.

Courtney asked me a question and then a few more followed, quizzing my pageant knowledge. After I rambled answers that didn't make any sense I knew it didn't take her long to figure out she had a beginner contestant to coach.

"One last question, Lucy. How is your support team? I see your mom is with you today." She smiled at Mom.

"Team?"

"How does your husband feel about you competing?"

"He's great about it."

Courtney gave me a suspicious look. "Really? Most wives I coach aren't so fortunate. Husbands are fearful their wives' needs and wants in life will change after being on stage. They'll become restless in their marriage and desire someone or something more exciting than them."

"No, Tom's great with everything." I forced a smile. *I definitely wasn't going to tell her about Claudia not supporting the idea.*

"Lucy, you are doing the right thing by hiring me. Not only will I coach you to victory, but I will help you build a team of people who will be your support system of which I will be a part. Let's begin. I see you brought your wardrobe."

The three of us stood and I unzipped the wardrobe bag and handed it to Mom. I held up my interview suit to showcase it, like the *Deal or No Deal* models.

Courtney walked around it, "Hmm, I see…" tapping her lips with her index finger three times.

Impressive. Even her fingernail polish was a cream color, but did she love the suit or hate it?

Lowering her voice she explained, "Your interview outfit looks like a mother-of-a-bride suit or something that a forty-year-old loan officer would wear." Courtney circled me once more. "The color is dull, hemline too long, the jacket is boxy with shoulder pads. Not at all pageant wear."

I glanced at Mom for her reaction. Her shoulders dropped and sadness clouded her eyes. She sat down and my hopes unraveled.

Going into inspirational speech mode, Courtney said, "Your first impression will make an important statement. This outfit does not portray success. It does not shout, 'I'm a winner.'"

The fog lifted. Courtney wasn't killing my hopes. She was molding me.

"Your suit must pop with color. The skirt should be a few inches above the knee, the blazer fitted and contoured to your body. That means a trip to an expert tailor, Lucy, and I have a name and phone number for you. She is worth the expense. Believe me. Seemingly insignificant details done wrong are like a neon sign to the judges. You don't want one letter to flicker."

Courtney proceeded with the list of to-dos.

Sweat trickled down between my breasts. My suit had already taken one trip to the tailor for shortening. I couldn't return it now.

"The suit needs a delicate, feminine neck-line but not so low that it would embarrass a judge." Courtney outlined her chest with her finger. "It is a pageant for married women, after all. It is in the small details." She continued with her I-know-my-stuff attitude. "You must finish the outfit with appropriate earrings, pageant shoes and no matter what do not have VPLs!"

"Pageant shoes? VPLs? What are they?" I felt dumber by the minute.

"Visible panty lines, huge no-no's."

"How do I keep my panty lines from showing? Go without?"

"Yes, go without. Or you can wear thongs, panty hose with a built in cotton panty, or my favorite, a body slimmer. It helps flatten your tummy and create a smooth waist-to-thigh silhouette."

"I don't think I'd be comfortable going without."

"You really are new to this, aren't you?" Courtney giggled, her emerald green eyes sparkled. "For your interview your shoes need a heel that makes you look taller, slimmer and flatters your leg shape. They should be a neutral color so they don't draw attention to your feet. Earrings should not be too long, they might distract. You want the judge to look you in the eyes and long earrings could be what he or she remembers, instead of your lovely face. No noisy bracelets, as they can distract also. Wear jewelry which complements the outfit instead of overpowering it. If in doubt you should under-accessorize."

I glanced over at Mom her pencil moving as fast as Courtney talked. Of course she was taking notes and I was thankful. I should have brought a tape recorder.

I was numb. I couldn't feel my fingertips or toes. I was confused about the criticism she made about my interview suit. Trying to make sense of everything, I thought I heard Courtney use the words "dull, old fashioned and maternal." Everything was wrong.

Okay, it did make me look maternal. What other kind of suit was there? I had searched for information about the so-called rules of the pageant, and I hadn't found any.

All the money and energy I put into shopping was wasted. I had to do it all over again. Tears welled up.

Slim chance Tom will support me if I keep spending money, as if I were the Queen of England, instead of a small town princess of a Mrs. Oregon beauty pageant.

Ninety minutes ticked by. "That's a wrap for today. It looks like we will need a few more sessions."

Unable to find my voice my head nodded automatically in agreement, glad that Courtney was willing to continue working with me.

"We only touched on the subject of your interview suit. You do have an evening gown, right?"

I nodded again.

"Next week we'll look at your evening gown. The week after that, we'll go shopping and finish up your wardrobe. Plan an all-day trip, because we're going to the big city."

"The big city?"

"Portland."

I couldn't afford that.

The time with Courtney flew by for me. I paid for her time and expertise before Mom and I left her beautiful home.

During the long silent drive home, given the new revelation on my suit, I tightened my grip on the steering wheel wavering if I should drop the whole idea, Operation Pageant was imploding. My mind flitted to Tom. He would be happy if I quit now. He wouldn't have to make excuses or explain to Claudia why I was away from home and the children, chasing an unreachable adventure and spending his money.

My fantasy of standing center stage, microphone in hand, with the spotlight on me was fading fast. I felt like a dandelion that had gone to seed. One puff and my hopes scattered in the wind. One poof and my dream was gone.

Mom spoke and jolted me out of my thoughts.

"Tiara was cute."

"Yep." I kept my eyes straight ahead.

"I'm glad we found out now about your interview suit, aren't you? Can you imagine if you showed up to compete and saw what all the other women were wearing? I'm sure there will be lots of contestants who will be wearing the wrong outfit."

"I had no idea this was so hard." I continued to look straight ahead, afraid if I looked at Mom, I would cry. "We spent hours, energy and money to purchase that suit. Now, I find out it's all wrong, And, I liked it. That's the scary part."

"I wonder what Courtney will say about your evening dress." Mom kidded, trying to keep things light.

"That's probably all wrong too." I squeezed out a chuckle.

"Oh no. It won't be. I love your evening gown. It's beautiful."

"There goes our idea of a black and white theme."

Mom didn't respond.

It was dusk when I dropped her off at her house, and dark by the time I parked beside Tom's car in the driveway. The last thing I wanted right now was to answer questions about how my day went. I hoped the kids would be rambunctious and demand my attention, so I could dodge Tom's questions.

~SIX~
Seeing Color

The ringing persisted as I closed the lid to the washing machine and tried to determine the location of the phone. I dashed through the main rooms, pausing to listen. Nope, not there. Drat. Where was that phone? I stood frozen, listened, then scurried again. Someday I would get organized, I vowed to the organizing gods. Six rings. Found it. "Hello…hello. I huffed and puffed.

"Lucy?"

"Oh good. You didn't hang up Tom, I'm glad you're still there."

"Of course I didn't hang up. I envisioned you running around the house frantically searching for the phone." He laughed. "Where was it this time? Behind the toilet seat?"

"Ha, ha, very funny. What's up?" I walked back into the utility room and pushed the start button on the washing machine.

"Lucy, I just received a husband's letter from the pageant to my work address."

Uh-oh, this can't be good. I clutched the phone tighter between my shoulder and ear. "You did?"

"Did you know I have to record a heartfelt message to you? The pageant plays it out loud for the audience to hear while you model your evening gown on stage. And I have to escort you. On stage! And I have to rent a tux. And I have to buy you flowers. And there is a husband's rehearsal. And did I say I have to be on stage?" Tom barely paused for a breath. "What did you get me into?" His voice sounded tired.

I had no idea how to respond as fingernails scraped the blackboard of my brain. This was the first I had heard about the husband's involvement in the pageant. "I'm sorry, Honey. I didn't know." *I hope he doesn't insist I stop now and back out because of his added role.*

"I feel sick to my stomach. You know how I hate being the center of attention," Tom said.

"Back in the day we thrived on attention. Which is why you married me." I waited for him to snuff out my dreams like a quick breeze over a candle. Yet another blackened wick for my collection of dreams.

"You are writing my message for me. You are ordering my tux. And you are picking out your own flowers."

Phew! At least he agreed to do it. "Okay, sweetheart, no problem." I hung up before he could change his mind. I left the utility room, rubbing the knot in my neck that formed in the last moments, and passed through the kitchen. Still clutching the phone, I dialed Courtney. "This is Lucy. Is this an okay time for you to talk?"

"Yes, of course. Are you calling to set up a time to go over the evening gown portion of the competition?"

It was like she could read my mind. "Yes, I'll bring my gown. Also, there is another reason for my call," I paused, and she waited for me to continue. "Tom just found out he has a significant role in this pageant." I couldn't hide my disappointment.

"And he's not happy about it." She finished my sentence.

"No, not really, he's going to do it though."

"The best thing you can do is to let him know he is number one in your life and your marriage is worth more to you than any pageant. Remember, this is a pageant for *married* women."

I looked at the family photos on the wall. Smiling faces, mine increasingly chubbier, as the years progressed.

"You need *all* of his support. He's part of your team."

"Thank you. I needed to hear that."

"Now how about meeting tomorrow at nine?"

"That works. Can I bring the pageant paperwork? There is a bio form I have to fill out for the judges and I received information about ad-pages that I don't understand."

"Sure. See you tomorrow."

"Thanks. See you at nine." I let out a breath of air and the tension in my neck was gone.

~

Mom fell in step alongside me as we walked toward Courtney's front door. My evening gown slung over my arm, and the paperwork secured in a three-ring binder I had organized before my coaching appointment. We entered Courtney's great room once again. Her Victorian décor was neat and clean as it had been during our last visit. My attention shifted to her wall mounted flat-screen television with a glamorous pageant scene paused.

"Is that you?" I walked closer to the screen.

Mom looked over at the television.

"That pageant was four years ago." Courtney's words hung like she wanted to reminisce. She stopped herself from twirling her hair like a teenage girl, then bent over and picked up Tiara instead. "I won that year." Courtney swiped her hand through the air and then scratched little Tiara behind her ear.

"That gown is beautiful, and…you…you're gorgeous." I moved forward to see the details. My heart flooded with admiration. I marveled at Courtney poised on the screen.

She stepped in front of me to put Tiara down. From nowhere she pulled out a long, thin, metal wand, similar to those used by orchestra conductors.

I glanced at Mom, took a step back, and winced.

Mom appeared to be holding back a laugh, though I believed I heard a tiny snort. I wasn't sure if it was because of the scared expression on my face, or Courtney's wand magically appearing. Either way, Mom's smile put me at ease.

Courtney's eyes narrowed as she pointed her wand at the forty-eight-inch plasma screen. "Right here." She placed the tip of the wand to the bottom of her gown. "You will notice my hemline. It is the perfect length. If yours is too short, you will look ridiculous. However, do not allow your gown to be so long it drags on stage. Your hemline should kiss the top of your shoe." Courtney kissed her fingers like an Italian chef preparing the perfect entrée.

"I can remember that."

Courtney raised her wand to the screen and made a circular motion around the chest area. "Do not have a neckline slit to the naval or excessive cleavage. Enough said?"

"Of course. I understand."

Moving the wand down the screen to the bodice, Courtney continued, "You may need to alter the gown to ensure it will contour your figure."

She doesn't know I already altered my gown and it cost plenty.

Courtney lowered the wand to her side and gave me the once over. "I see you're a little on the…the hippy side, and you are short. How tall are you? Five-foot five?"

"Yeah, I mean, yes." I lowered my head. "I've been running and working out."

"You need a gown with vertical lines to create a long, narrow silhouette. Draw the judge's eye upward, with detailing at the neck. As for the hips avoid belts, waistbands, and bows. A straight gown tends to look best."

She moved the wand behind her back and her other arm joined it. She took a stance that suggested her closing remarks about the evening gown were soon to come.

"The woman who wins is the woman who makes the least mistakes throughout the pageant. Judges look for poise, class, grace, elegance, and a gown that complements her personality."

Mom whipped out her notebook again, knowing I wouldn't remember all of Courtney's advice. We would review her notes in the car on the way home. As she wrote, she mouthed the words "poise, class, and elegance."

I smiled at her determination to help me.

"Go for the crown. Carry yourself like a queen, and be a winner!" Courtney pushed the red button on the remote. "Now, go try on your evening gown."

Mom chatted with Courtney while I stepped into the spacious bathroom to change. The bright, pink wallpaper had silver tiaras sporadically imprinted on the paper.

Did her husband even live in this house?

I undressed and fumbled with the zipper on my gown.

In the living room, Mom asked Courtney "Is there a certain color which is better than another?"

"Yes, a contestant should choose a color that is correct for her hair and skin tone. One color may make her pale, or cast a yellow or green shade on her face, while another color will make her look radiant."

"What color would you recommend for Lucy?"

"With her strawberry red hair, you can't go wrong with white. White conveys clean, innocence, lady-like, and pure. The word is, white wins pageants, but that is only a myth."

Mom continued scribbling as fast as Courtney was speaking.

"I would also recommend for her hair color and pale skin tone hunter green, medium pastel aqua, turquoise and with her being full through the hips, black."

"Black. Great that's the color that Lucy bought. You'll see in a second." Mom said, a cheerful note in her voice.

"Black reads sophistication, glamour, maturity, and elegance, whereas, blues might say calm, conservative, and dignified. It depends on what message you want to convey to the judges."

"What colors should Lu stay away from?" Mom asked questions like a news journalist after a hot story.

"There are exceptions to every pageant rule. Generally I would stay away from brown, gray, camel, mustard, olive green, orange and dark purple."

I stepped out of Courtney's pink pampered powder room wearing my midnight black gown.

There was a long silence.

Mom stiffened and held her breath while we waited to hear what Courtney had to say.

Oh brother, here we go again.

"I see." Courtney said. "Black is okay, but this gown is all wrong." She shook her head. "It looks like you're going to your high school prom or on vacation on a cruise line, not a pageant." There was no sorry in her voice. "I'll help you find another gown when we shop for your new interview suit."

"What do you suggest I look for?" I stared at my new, high-heeled shoes.

"You must avoid purchasing clothes with prints or those which are too loud. You want the judges to see you as a person. You want them to remember you and not the dress."

"I'm sorry I don't know more about pageants." I lowered my eyes. "I didn't realize there was so much to it."

"Don't worry. That's why I'm here. I see this frequently with first-time contestants. Let me show you one of my gowns, so you can see the difference." Courtney returned from a closet designated for her pageant wardrobe and returned with a pale blue sequined, glitzy, glamorous, body-hugging gown.

The difference was obvious. I wanted to try it on, but didn't dare ask. Besides I'm sure I wouldn't have been able to squeeze into it.

"Our time is over. We didn't get to your paperwork. I think we should have weekly coaching sessions. Does every Tuesday at nine work for you?"

"Yes, that works." I turned toward the bathroom to change out of my *all wrong* gown.

Mom flipped through her planner, penciling in nine on every Tuesday.

How am I going to pay for all of these sessions? I forced the problem out of my mind, gathered my belongings, and we said goodbye.

With silence in the car, once again, I held back tears. Through the windshield I spied a familiar blue and red sign. "Want to go through Dairy Queen's drive thru?" I asked softly. "I could use a triple chocolate blizzard right now."

"Sure, I'm always up for some chocolate," Mom patted my thigh. "Things will get easier, Honey."

If only Mom knew. Things were about to get tougher once I told Tom I needed another new pageant wardrobe.

~SEVEN~
My Queen

When I rolled the SUV to a stop, weariness gripped me. I sat behind the wheel looking through the living room window.

Tom came to the door and glanced at his watch. I figured it probably wasn't the first time that night he had checked the time, since he was already out of his slacks and dress shirt and into his favorite pair of faded denim jeans and Oregon sweatshirt.

Tom stepped outside to meet me, as I shifted our vehicle into park. He opened my door.

The moon peeked through the tree branches lighting our path and a cool breeze played with my hair.

"Finally." Tom's eyes were troubled.

"Yeah. Sorry. Rough day." I shook my head. "Everything is going wrong that can go wrong. I'm not doing anything right for this pageant." I refused to cry. I body-bumped the car door, it shut hard and I shuddered at the echo of the slam.

"Why don't you quit then?" Tom turned his gaze toward the trees.

"Quit? I didn't say I wanted to quit. It's been a rough day is all I said." I stomped a few feet toward the house. "Why? Do you want me to quit?"

"No, I was just saying, if you want to quit it would be no big deal." Tom threw his hands up.

"No big deal, huh? Well, it's a big deal to me." I turned and glared at him. "I get it. You don't want me to compete, huh?"

"I didn't say that."

"Well, Tom Rupp, I'm no quitter. I am going to compete and I am going to win! You just wait and see." I swiped my bangs from my eyes as the wind rearranged my hair. "I'm paying for a coach. I subscribe to the pageant magazine. I'm watching every pageant on television. No one is working harder on this pageant than me. So, yes I am going to compete and I am going to win."

"Where did you go after you left Courtney's? I've been waiting for you."

I didn't answer.

"I asked you a question. Where have you been?"

Tom stepped past me and looked through the driver's side window. He chuckled, then laughed, "Ah ha! Just as I thought. Evidence from Dairy Queen." He smirked before continuing, "Well, well…you're not going to win the swimsuit portion of the pageant, Lucy, if you keep drowning your sorrows in chocolate." Tom stepped back from the window, grabbed my hips, and yanked me in for a tight hug.

I relaxed, joined in his laughter and slipped my arms around his waist.

"I wasn't drowning my sorrows," I whispered into his chest.

"Yes, you were. And you know it." He lowered his voice. "Don't try and hide it from me, Lu." Tom placed his finger under my jaw line, tilted my chin upward, and added a slight kiss on my lips. "Let's go inside. You can share your terrible day with me. I'll get your gown out of the back seat."

"Thanks, Babe. Alright just so you know you really do know me. I *was* drowning my sorrows."

He swung my gown over his shoulder and kicked the back car door shut.

"Thanks for understanding me so well. I love you."

"Listen, Lu. I don't need any pageant judge to tell me you're the most beautiful woman in the whole wide world. I could care less what some judge thinks of you."

His words melted my heart like hot butter drizzled on popcorn.

I wished Tom had let the conversation end at that but he continued to speak. "Since you insist and you are going to spend all of this time and money to find out what others think of you, then I guess we'll have to go through this dumb pageant experience."

"Find out what others think of me? Dumb? Did Claudia say that?" I waited for him to respond.

He was silent.

"You don't understand. That's typical of you. Let's not argue. Let's call this conversation over." I huffed and walked quickly to the house.

"Perfect, just perfect! That's just like you, Lucy." Tom raised his voice with each word. "You never want to finish a conversation, do you?"

"There is nothing more to talk about. So yes, this conversation is over. I'm tired. I'm going to bed. You put the kids down." I stormed up the steps and didn't look back.

I opened the front door and a gentle ocean wave of quiet peace came over me and pulled me in. The sea of toys was picked up, floor vacuumed, dishes done and the clean laundry put away. Soft music played and crackling came from the blazing fireplace. A beautiful bouquet of red roses with an envelope attached stood proudly on the dining room table.

A soft gasp dropped out of my mouth. *I had just yelled at the man who did this.* I opened the envelope with my name written on it.

The card read: *You are my queen! Love, Tom*

~EIGHT~
Aahhh!

Rays of sunshine fanned through the cracks of our blinds. The warmth of the sunlight landed on my cheek. I rolled out of bed, stretching like a lazy cat.

"Hello, sunshine," I greeted the morning. I looked at the clock on Tom's nightstand. He had left for work over an hour ago.

"Today is a new day," I told myself. "I'm going to give my family a well-deserved break from listening to me obsess about the pageant. I'm not going to bring up the topic even once."

Full of energy and purpose, I phoned Tom at work. "Are you going to be home on time tonight? I want to prepare a special dinner."

"That would be great, Lu. I'll invite The Gang and Claudia."

"Tom! Not Claudia. She doesn't fit in. Remember what happened last time? She criticized our friends and left them speechless."

"You're right. I just thought it would be a nice gesture."

"It is a nice gesture. Just not a good idea."

"Okay, I'll help with the preparations."

"That would be great. Um, Hon, I'm in the mood for salmon and fresh vegetables."

Courtney had said, "Eating right means losing weight."

"So, you're saying not our usual BBQ tonight?" Tom confirmed.

Good, no disagreement. No fuss over the cost.

"Right. I'm in the mood for fish."

"Okay, the change will be nice." Tom added.

"So, you will swing by the grocery store?"

"Yep, no problem. See ya later."

"Also pick up hot dogs for the kids."

I placed the phone back on the cradle and walked past my jewelry box. I didn't have the time, but I picked through my costume jewelry. What could I use for pageant weekend? I knew I shouldn't get distracted from cleaning my house before company arrived, but I had a mission. Piece by piece, I carefully laid out necklaces, earrings, and bracelets on the pretty bedspread. Some pieces were tarnished and chipped. The heart-shaped pendants were more suited for Suzy to play with than for a pageant queen to wear. My heart sank. *Nothing would work.*

What was I going to do?

More shopping, more money, more rationalizing, more "I'm sorry, Tom."

~

Pete, Julie and their two children were first to arrive for dinner. Julie climbed out of the car holding an almond cherry cake, everyone's favorite dessert. Their kids ran past me, through the house, out the back door. They joined Adam, Jake, and Suzy playing Monopoly and waited for hot dogs, pork and beans, and potato chips at the picnic table.

"I'm glad I didn't have to bake today. Thanks, Jules." I smelled the almond flavor in the cake. "The Gang will love you." I took the plate from her hands and walked into the kitchen. I mumbled to the diet gods, "Please give me the will power to pass on it."

Selena and Ron arrived, and directly behind them, Colleen and Mark.

"Hi, guys. I'm glad you could come for dinner. I know it was short notice." I propped the door open with my hip.

"That's the best kind of notice." Ron took off his extra-large jacket, hung it in the closet, and gave me a quick hug.

"Where's Sandra and David?" I asked.

"They should be right behind us." Colleen glanced over her shoulder.

"Dinner won't be much longer. Tom is in the kitchen working on the meal."

"I'll go say hi to the old guy." Ron bolted from the living room.

"I'm leaving you girls out here to do your girl talk," Mark added and fell in step behind Ron.

The house grew noisy with everyone laughing, chatting and enjoying each other's company. The men talked about their jobs and the ladies chatted about the latest sales at Macy's. The aroma of salmon caused my stomach to growl, reminding me I hadn't eaten much today.

"There's Sandra and David," Selena looked out the front window.

David stepped into the house. "I could smell dinner from outside."

"Dinner's ready," I shouted over everyone talking.

No one seemed to hear me.

"Ooo-eee!" Ron patted his stomach and let out a belly laugh.

What was that all about?

All the women gravitated toward the snappy comments and jokes from the men.

Pete, Ron, Mark, and David, stood around the dining room table, their heads together like they were in a football huddle discussing the next great play. They stared at the bouquet of red roses in the middle of the table.

"You old romantic." David sniffed once and slapped Tom on the back.

I stiffened, watching the men, bracing myself for what Tom's friends might say.

"Tom, you're making all of us look bad, you dawg." Peter plucked a single rose out of the vase, put the stem between his teeth, raised his hand over his head, snapped his fingers and performed a Spanish hat dance around the dining room table.

"Pete, stop that. Those are *my* roses." I giggled, feeling my cheeks turn red.

Now everyone gathered in the kitchen. The wives pushed their husbands to the side, so they could see what the fuss was about. There was a chorus of "oohs" and "ahhs" from my girlfriends.

"Those are beautiful. What's the occasion?" Julie asked.

"It's not your birthday or anniversary. What did Tom do? Colleen fingered a rose petal.

Sandra nudged David with her elbow. "You should take a lesson from Tom."

"So, what's the occasion?" Selena repeated Julie's question and grabbed for the card on the plastic stick in the middle of the bouquet.

I wished I had thought to hide the card. I glanced at Tom, biting my lower lip. *I'm sorry you got busted for being a romantic.*

"You are my queen," Selena read out loud. "Aaahh."

"Come on, you guys, dinner is ready. Let's all gather around, and Pete, you say grace." I tried to herd them to their seats and change the subject.

"Oh no, Lu, not so fast," Julie said.

Selena, with her slender fingers, picked grapes from the bowl and popped them into her mouth one by one, chewing and smiling, at the same time enjoying the entertainment.

"Yeah, spill the beans," Colleen added.

"Or grapes." Selena shrugged and reached for another.

Everyone laughed. The kitchen became eerily silent and all eyes aimed at me.

I looked at Tom with pleading eyes, giving him a nod of reassurance that it was okay for him to tell The Gang about the pageant.

"Well…" Tom cleared his throat, taking command of the floor. "My beautiful, sweet, most gorgeous wife in the whole world is going to compete in a pageant for married women this spring." Everyone turned and looked at me. "The roses are to tell her, no matter what the outcome, she is my queen, today and forever."

Silence. Then the kitchen erupted with congratulatory comments from my friends.

During dinner they asked questions about the pageant. Julie seemed the most interested.

Just above a whisper, Julie said, "I have always wanted to enter a pageant."

What? She wanted to be in a pageant?

She was, after all, the one who pointed out Mrs. Oregon in church, way back when.

I caught Tom's eye in the middle of the noisy chatter and mouthed, "Thank you."

He winked.

The night ended. Our friends all promised to come to the pageant, hold up signs with my name in glitter and support me on my big night. I closed the door behind everyone and gave Tom a huge hug.

"What's that for?"

I squeezed him tighter. "Thank you, babe, for what you said before dinner." I let go and took a step back. "Do you *really* think I'm beautiful, sweet, and gorgeous?"

"Why don't I show you how I *really* feel right now?" He wiggled an eyebrow.

"Yes, why don't you?" I grabbed his wrist and pulled him into the bedroom.

~NINE~
Carry Yourself Like a Queen

Please, Tom. I need you to stay home tomorrow and watch the kids. There's no school." I folded my arms.

"I can't, Lucy. You know every Tuesday is office meetings. My attendance is mandatory and I have a house closing afterwards." His tone was unwavering. "I never miss a closing."

My shoulders slumped. "What am I going to do?"

"Call Claudia. She'd love to watch the kids."

"No way. She'll ask why and you know how she feels about the pageant. Besides, then I'd have to listen to her lecture me on not being home with the kids. I'm begging you, please."

"Call your mom, then."

"I already told you, Mom is coming with me."

"You don't have a choice." He walked to the phone. "Here, I'll even call Claudia for you."

"Can you at least drop the kids off at her house in the morning so I don't have to face her? I'll get them ready," I clasped my hands together and batted my eyes.

"Okay, I can do that."

~

Spring break was evident everywhere. When I stepped outside splashes of color among the full bloom blanket of tulips and daffodils awakened my senses. Mom and I drove to my nine o'clock coaching appointment, like every Tuesday since I began this adventure. We walked up the pebble sidewalk to Courtney's home. A yellow Post-it note was stuck on the door and in elegant handwriting stated, *Lucy, walk around the house to the backyard.*

"What's going on?" Mom asked.

I handed her the note before we turned and stepped down the stairs. The smell of fresh-cut grass enveloped us as we hurried to the backyard. I hoped Mom wasn't getting tired of the arduous pageant process. I hadn't told her today how much I appreciated the trips, shopping sprees, and late night phone calls.

I rose on my tiptoes to blindly feel for the latch on the other side of the gate, my hand searching until I released the metal bar. I grinned like I was on a game show. What was behind Door Number One? I swung open the tall, heavy gate then we stepped into the backyard.

Courtney walked back and forth on a homemade runway built on top of her luscious, well-groomed, oversized lawn. She wore a pair of four-inch high heels, like the famous Victoria Secret Angels.

As we watched her, I sucked in a deep breath and soaked in the sight of the park-like backyard, which included a dollhouse for their pampered dog, complete with Tiara's name printed in script on a crown-shaped sign.

"Amazing." My eyes widened. "Who does that?"

"She does take pageants seriously, doesn't she?" Mom said under her breath.

Courtney called out from the runway, "This is where I teach and practice the walk. The on-stage walk." Courtney extended her hands palms up, and sang, "Ta-daaa!"

I thought I had walked onto a movie set. I gave Courtney a Hollywood smile.

My mom seemed to think everything was normal because she said, "Hello. You have a beautiful backyard."

"Thank you. Did you remember your high heels, Lucy?"

"Uh-huh." I gulped. "I mean, *yes*."

Thank you, Mom, for insisting we go over the list of things I needed to bring today.

"Great. Slip them on. I'll teach you how to walk, stop, and turn on stage. When I coach women who are entering their first pageant, their pace is much too fast. They all walk the runway like they're on fire and dashing toward water." Courtney snickered.

"Own the stage, take your time, and you will look confident. Confidence is becoming. People will notice." Courtney straightened her back and continued. "Another common mistake is arching your back too much. That makes you look stiff." She turned in the middle of the runway. "You should glide like you're on ice skates."

With practice, and more practice, could I be graceful like her?

Mom meandered across the yard, distracted by the array of spring flowers. She touched, smelled, and cooed over Courtney's garden. For once, I wished she were taking notes.

"First things first. Never slouch, slump, or hang your head." Courtney stood erect. "Walk with grace and poise. Pretend to float on air, arms relaxed at your sides, fingertips ever so slightly brushing your thighs, until you master the walk. Don't swing your arms out too wide, or hold them too stiff." Courtney walked up and down her runway to demonstrate. She made it look easy and natural.

I glanced at Mom, now further down the fence line in her own little world, enjoying all the flowers. I wanted her attention.

Mom, take notes.

"And one more thing. Do not do what I call 'the gun.'" Courtney raised her index finger with her thumb out and blew on it.

"The gun?" I copied her gesture.

"A lot of women are nervous, so they hold their hands and point their fingers like a gun." Courtney held up her right hand in a gun position and pointed it toward me, then lowered her hand, pointer finger to the ground. "Never do that."

I listened intently and watched.

"Step up here and practice walking and turning." She helped me onto the runway.

"Mom, watch me," I called out like a five-year-old riding a bicycle for the first time without training wheels.

What would it feel like, standing high above an audience with eyes following me, the crowd clapping and whistling?

"Good, Lucy. That's good. Here's another tip. Walk with a radiant smile and the judges will look at your face and not at your feet. When you get to the end of the runway, stand in the ten and twelve position. I'll show you."

"Ten and what?" I turned to hear her repeat how to stand.

"Pretend you are standing in the center of a clock. Like this." Courtney stood with her back foot pointing at ten on the imaginary timepiece and her front foot pointing at twelve. Tiara bounced between her legs and nipped at her ankles. "You try it," she encouraged.

I stood with my feet apart and turned one foot out.

"Okay, now slide your twelve o'clock heel back, until it touches the inside arch in your ten o'clock foot, forming a T. Rotate your hips slightly to face forward."

"Like this?" I tottered on my heels.

"That's not bad. When you exit the stage, keep eye contact with the judges until the last second. Keep your posture and smile until you are completely behind the curtain and they can no longer see you. Many times, women think the judges are not watching, but believe me, the judges are still evaluating you as you exit. Never let down for a second."

Mom finally walked back to the stage, and now I had her complete attention. I walked up and down the runway, listened to Courtney, and tried to be graceful as I wobbled in my uncomfortable, too-high heels.

"That's right. Now, every day I want you to put on your high heels and practice walking for fifteen minutes. *Every day*. Remember to carry yourself like a queen." Courtney spoke with conviction.

My knees shook and my feet ached. *I wanted a break and work on something else, like my bio.*

"Okay, Lucy. You can stop. We're done with part one of today's lesson.

Finally, a rest.

"Let's go inside and start on your paperwork." Courtney led the way through the back yard's sliding glass door into her kitchen.

While Mother admired Courtney's bamboo dining room table, my gaze was drawn to the life-size portrait of Courtney. It hung on the wall next to the elegant bamboo china hutch, which matched the dining room table. She wore a long white dress, held a bouquet of white roses, and a beautiful crown encircled her head.

"Would you like some ice tea?"

"That would be wonderful," Mom answered.

"Uh-huh. Yes. I would love some too." I studied her portrait, and imagined I would have a similar one hanging in my home someday.

Courtney set the ice tea in front of us.

I opened my three-ring notebook to the sheet of paper titled, *Bio for Judges.*

Courtney took a seat next to me and scooted her chair closer. "Be your best on paper. That's our goal for the second half of your lesson today. Think of this bio," Courtney patted the sheet of paper, "as an application for a job that could change your life. You need to sell yourself and help the judges familiarize themselves with you."

I tipped a teaspoon of sugar into my tea and thought about my accomplishments. "Does birthing three kids count?" Mom and I laughed.

Courtney didn't.

"Let me make some copies of your form. We can use them as practice sheets." Courtney said.

I snapped open the metal rings of my binder and handed the papers to Courtney.

"Excuse me, I'll be right back."

I whispered to Mom, "Do you think I could be like her? She's perfect."

"Lucy, stop comparing yourself to her and just be you."

"I still have to lose weight, learn to walk, buy special makeup—" I wasn't finished with my list when Courtney returned and handed the forms to me.

"When we finish filling out the forms, you will take them home and complete your bio. Never hand-write it. It needs to be impeccable. No errors." Courtney instructed.

I nodded okay, while squeezing a lemon into my tea.

"Let's start with hobbies."

"She likes to collect Star Wars memorabilia. Does that count?" Mom chimed in.

Oh-my-gosh-Mom, I couldn't believe she said that.

"No, collecting things usually doesn't count, unless they are very rare or have an interesting educational background, or maybe a lot of sentimental value."

I guess my collection of dust bunnies didn't count either.

"I used to enter road races, before I had kids."

"That's a start. Let's say you are a long-distance runner in charity fundraising marathons."

"Wow, that's great. I like it." I smiled and twirled the long spoon around in my glass, feeling better about my biography. I suppressed the guilt over the fib.

If Mom noticed, she didn't show it. "She likes to read," Mom said.

"That's good. What types of books?" Courtney asked.

"Autobiographies and inspirational books." I sat up straight and slid my glasses back up the arch of my nose out of habit.

"Okay. We'll put autobiographies of great Americans," Courtney said. "Make sure you know some titles of books you've read, because a judge may ask you what your favorite autobiography is. If you don't have an answer, they will think you puffed up your bio."

Wasn't that what we were doing?

"She volunteers, too," Mom said.

"Oh, that's wonderful. Yes, definitely write that as one of your accomplishments. Where do you volunteer?"

"I'm on the budget committee for our school district, and I'm involved with the PTA, Booster Club, and KidSports, though I haven't been to any meetings in the past seven months." I fidgeted with my spoon.

"The only thing the judges will know about you is what you type on that bio form. Make sure you know *exactly* what you have written. Bring a copy of the bio with you during pageant weekend, so you can review it before you start your private interviews. They take place earlier in the day, before you ever go on stage."

"Okay." I sipped my ice tea.

"What the judges read on your bio is what you are going to be asked about. Be prepared. There are four main questions judges usually ask."

Mom, ready with a pen.

"One, why did you enter this pageant? Two, where do you see yourself in five years? Three, what is your goal, if you win the state title for your year's reign? Last, what is your platform?"

While on autopilot, I nodded, placing my fingertips to my temples. Maybe the pressure would scare away the headache I felt coming on.

"Do you have a platform, Lucy? Something that passionately drives you? Your platform should show your compassion, commitment, and concern. It should show how you are improving the corner of the world where you live."

Courtney glanced at me. "Have you given this some thought? A platform is a very important matter."

"Yes, I'm actually excited and proud about my platform decision." I was prepared, for once. I sat straight in my chair, folded my hands together, and rested them on the table. "It's early intervention for children who are developmentally delayed in speech and language." I stopped for a second, gauging Courtney's reaction.

She smiled. "That's nice, Lucy. Something different than world peace. It's interesting. I can see it's a platform you are passionate about. The judges will notice your genuine enthusiasm during your interview." She went to the sliding glass door, opened it, and snapped her fingers three times.

Tiara popped out from around the corner and ran outside.

I continued to speak with a newfound confidence. "This is something I am very familiar with. It has affected me my entire life. You know, lack of verbal skills and all…in the English language." I took another sip of ice tea, while I waited for Courtney's affirmation. "I deal with this obstacle in my life on a daily basis."

"Great platform, Lucy." Courtney clapped her hands. "I like it."

Big sigh of relief.

"You should have a platform that personally touches your life in one way or another. You need to believe in it, because you will speak about it often. Platforms give direction and purpose to your title. It guides many appearances and speaking engagements throughout the year, and lends validity to your title."

Mom reached over and patted my forearm. For the first time, something had come naturally to me in this adventure.

"Time's up, Lucy, but before you leave, I want to assign some homework. Once a week, until your pageant, I want you to give speeches in your community about your platform. I don't care if it's an audience of three people or three hundred people. Just start giving speeches. Contact schools, churches, and local clubs, and ask if you can give a fifteen-minute speech about your subject. Also, think about joining a Toastmasters group."

I nodded, but…how could I spend more time away from Tom, housework, and the kids?

"Public speaking is a skill which is learned. The more you do it, the more confident you become. You'll be judged on your speaking ability in your personal interview, as well as the on-stage question, so you want to be extremely comfortable."

I gulped air. "Excuse me." I rushed to her washroom, locked the door, and turned on the cold water. The color drained from my face.

I gripped the marble counter top and stared in the mirror. My bangs stuck to my forehead and my stomach rolled. *Speeches at schools, walking on stage in heels, personal interviews. What had I gotten myself into?* I splashed cold water on my flushed cheeks, finger-combed my bangs from my moist forehead, and steadied my breathing. *You can do this.*

With a faint smile, I rejoined Courtney and Mom. "Thanks for your help. I—"

Courtney interrupted, "Before we meet again, type your bio, set up some public speaking arrangements, and research your platform. Learn statistics, facts, and percentages about your subject. Judges love to hear numbers. It confirms your commitment to your platform and passion for your cause."

My mind spun with information.

"Also, more homework. Here is a list of fifty questions. The judges might ask any one of these, so prepare and answer for each."

I had to get out of there and breathe, just breathe.

Mom and I poured out our thank you's and handed Courtney her well-earned fee before we departed.

⁓

No one answered the door when I knocked, I let myself into Claudia's modest home. It was silent. Immaculate. The aroma of pot-roast led me to the kitchen. *Where is everyone?* I looked out the large bay window. Adam, Jake, and Suzy were working in the garden with Claudia.

I stood watching and tried to envision a time working with my kids in a garden, but couldn't because I never had a garden.

That doesn't make you a bad mom, Lucy.

Suzy looked up from pushing dirt around a newly planted vegetable seed, which Claudia had let her plant to call her own. Later in the season, when it sprouted, Suzy would have her own personal bragging rights.

Suzy saw me through the window and flung her arm up for a big wave.

I moseyed out to join them. "Hi, guys. Hi, Claudia. Thanks for watching them for me." I gave Claudia a warm smile.

"Look what I did, Mom." Jake said, holding a trowel.

"It's good for the kids to be outside breathing fresh air and not always inside watching cartoons all day long." Claudia made her point, harsh words masked with sweet charm. "Kids need to smell fresh flowers, hear birds chirp and use their imaginations. They can't exercise their minds if they are always cooped up in the house planted in front of the television."

I swear I will never have Claudia watch my kids again.

My jaw tightened, "Believe me, Claudia, the kids have very active imaginations."

"Yes, I guess they do. I caught Suzy pretending to be a *queen* today." She wiped dirt off her cheek. "Speaking of queen, how was your time with the pageant coach?"

I told Tom specifically not to tell her what I did today.

"It was fine. Thank you for watching the kids." I clenched my teeth.

"Anytime. I'm glad you didn't pay a babysitter. I'm sure this pageant is costing Tom a fortune."

"I don't need babysat." Adam threw his opinion into the conversation.

"No, Honey, you don't." I winked at him. "Come on, kids. Go get cleaned up." I nudged Suzy toward the house.

"You haven't talked to Tom yet? I invited everyone to stay for a home-cooked meal. I already called Tom and he said it would be fine. He should be here anytime."

"Oh, uh, okay, that'll be great." The kids seemed in no hurry to leave.

~TEN~
Junk In The Trunk

Claudia made it through dinner without mentioning the pageant.

Phew we made it through the pot roast, but dessert had yet to be served.

Her statements started, disguised as questions, when Claudia pushed the slice of five layer chocolate cake in front of me. "Why would anyone want to put themselves out in public to be judged?" and, "Aren't women who compete in pageants vain?" And my favorite, "These poor husbands who have to put up with these wives spending their money. How do they afford it? Have you thought about that, Lucy?"

I picked my way through eating the cake while I bluffed my way through answering her questions.

Why can't she support me? Why can't she be proud of me for trying something different?

Tom scooted his chair from the table. "Thanks sis, for dinner." He gave Claudia a peck on the cheek before he kicked up his feet in the living room and turned on the TV.

"Yes, thank you, it's nice to have the night off from cooking," I added. "I'll do the dishes. You relax and watch TV with Tom."

Anything to avoid getting stuck in the kitchen alone with her.

The next evening, I lay on the floor with my body pillow and my magazine, feet kicked up, music blasting through my earphones.

Tom leaned inside the doorway of our bedroom and waved his arms. "Lucy. Hey, Lu!"

"Yes." I tugged the earphones out of my ears and glanced over the top of the magazine.

"What are you doing, goof ball?" He kicked the bottom of my foot. "You're reading every word in that thing, aren't you? Including the small print at the bottom of each ad."

I glanced at my handsome husband with his tie loosened and his collar unbuttoned. "It's not a thing. It's a pageant magazine."

"Yeah, I know." Tom cocked his head, his mouth curved into a smirk. "Can you help me for a minute?

Tom fidgeted and shifted from side to side.

"Now?" I dog-eared my magazine so I wouldn't lose my place.

"Can you go into the office and find the receipts for the paint job on the house? The bookkeeper needs them. I've looked in there and can't seem to locate them."

"Did you look in the file cabinet?"

"Yes, but I couldn't find them. Please, just get off the pillow for two seconds and help me look." Tom stepped toward me and reached out to pull me up from the floor.

I trudged to the office, swung open the door and there, in the corner of the room, was a brand new treadmill decorated with a large red bow on top.

"Oh, Tom." I covered my mouth with both hands. "This is wonderful," My voice went up three octaves. "How did you get this? When did you get this? How did you get it into the house without me seeing it?" I jumped up and down and danced about the room.

Tom slapped his leg and did a fist pump, grinning from ear to ear. "I can't believe I pulled off a surprise." Tom cheered. "Pete helped me. I thought you might want a treadmill to help you get in shape for your pageant."

"I need all the help I can get." I laced my fingers behind my head and took a deep breath.

"With a treadmill, you can run any time of day, instead of early in the morning, before the kids wake up," Tom said. "Or before I wake up."

"I am the luckiest woman in the whole wide world. Thank you, Tom." I threw my arms around him. Just as suddenly, I stepped back, turned, and inspected the treadmill. "Can we afford this?"

Tom kissed the tip of my nose. "Don't worry about it. And, yes, we can afford it. I have another closing next week. By the way, it's your birthday gift too." Tom grinned.

"I don't care. It can be my Christmas, birthday, and Valentine's Day gift all rolled into one. I am so happy."

"What's all the noise about?" Jake came into the crammed office.

"Mommy found her treadmill," Suzy said, following Jake, carrying her Stevie Tenderheart doll by the hair. "Daddy said it's for her 'junk in her trunk.'"

"Tom!" I jerked to attention and held both hands in fists straight down. "You said that?" I offered a broad wink.

Suzy looked up at me. "Where's your trunk, mama?"

Tom swatted my rear, singing, "Junk in the trunk, junk in the trunk."

I scooted away from him.

He continued to swat my rear.

I scooted some more. My scoot became a jog around the office, through the maze of clutter, treadmill, and kids. The kids joined in, chasing me around, until our family looked like a choo-choo train.

Huffing and puffing, I made a sudden stop, spun, and wrapped my arms around Tom and squeezed. "Honey, thank you so much. It's just like you to always think of me. I love you."

"I love you too and just so you know, if you never lose your junk, I couldn't care less."

"I'm going to change into my sweats right now and try it out." I danced to our bedroom.

Minutes later I had my water bottle to the left, a towel to the right, and in the center, my pageant homework, fifty mock questions the panel of judges might ask.

I pushed the start button and waited for the belt to move. Slowly, one foot in front of the other, I matched its pace until I was walking. I was in the zone.

My eyes scanned the paper, searching for an easy question to begin answering and memorizing.

Name three things you did to prepare for this pageant.

"Hey, Tom," I hollered over the television in the living room.

"Is something wrong with the treadmill?" He paused the game and came in the office.

"No." I smiled. "Name three things I'm doing to prepare for this pageant."

Tom looked around the corner back at the television, "One, you spent money. Two, you spent money, and three, you spent more money."

"Tom. Seriously, a judge could ask me that question."

"Tell them how you lost weight by dieting and exercising."

"But, then I would have to admit I had to lose weight, and I don't want them to know that I ever had weight to lose."

"That thinking doesn't make sense, Lucy. It tells them you are a real woman with real issues, and you were able to overcome them. I'm sure it will be fine."

"Maybe. I'll think about it." I pushed the button to speed up the treadmill. "I can't tell them that, unless I lose more weight. Thank you again for the treadmill."

I muddled my way through several more questions until I was satisfied with a few practice answers.

Setting the treadmill speed to a slower walking pace, I continued to strategize my interview process. If I memorized five important things I wanted each judge to know about me, and then practiced finding ways I could loop, weave, and intertwine one of those five answers into every question, basically I would only need to have five answers memorized and pick one of those answers to match one of the fifty questions. Simple enough.

The phone rang. "Lucy, it's for you." Tom brought me the phone.

I slowed the treadmill, and pushed the off button.

"Who is it?" I mouthed, reaching to take the phone.

"I don't know," Tom mouthed back. Then he hovered like a cloud ready to dump its rain.

"Hello?" I tried not to pant into the receiver.

"Hello, is this Lucy?" a cheery-sounding male voice asked.

"Yes, this is Lucy."

"My name is Dusty Joe Westbrook, but sweetie, you can call me Dusty Joe."

"Uh-huh." I looked at Tom and shrugged.

"Courtney asked me to call you and set up an appointment for your pageant headshot."

"Oh, okay." I balanced the phone between my ear and shoulder and swiped the towel to dab the beads of sweat off my forehead.

"She's my girl, and I am her personal photographer. I work by referral only."

My brain tried to keep up with his fast-speaking pace.

"I have one opening available to do a photo shoot on Friday at three. Does that work for you?"

I imagined him studying his perfectly manicured fingernails as he spoke. "Oh, yes. Yes, it will. Thank you very much, Dusty Joe." I watched Tom's expression and wondered what he was thinking. I imagined a word bubble over his head filled with dollar signs and question marks.

"You're welcome. See you Friday at my studio."

"See you at three." I wiped the lingering sweat and makeup off the phone and handed it back to Tom.

"Dusty Joe? Who is that?" Tom widened his stance.

"Dusty Joe Westbrook." I said his name imitating his high-pitched tone. "Courtney had him call me to set up a photo shoot for the headshot I need for the judges' bio sheet and the pageant program book. I have an appointment with him on Friday."

"Friday?" Tom tilted his head. "Lu, any day but Friday." His voice lowered.

"What? Why not Friday?"

"How could you not remember?"

His question jabbed my heart.

~ELEVEN~
Picture Perfect

Standing in the doorway of the office with a hardened expression, Tom shoved one hand into his front pocket and ran the other through his thick, brown hair. "You forgot, I took the day off from work to take you out for your birthday. I have a special day planned for us. Call Dusty Joe back and change the date." Tom leaned back on the wall and folded his arms.

My heart twisted. I didn't want to hurt Tom. "I can't cancel, and I won't cancel."

"Why?" He glanced at the treadmill. "Why can't you, Lu?" He gritted his teeth.

I took a deep breath. "It's not that easy. You don't understand."

"Oh, let me guess. Because this pageant is the most important thing in your life right now, is that it? More important than me, huh?" His tone shifted to a sneer. "You can tell the judges the three things you did to prepare for this stupid pageant other than spending money and losing weight, is one you forgot who your husband is. Two, you forgot you have kids. And three, you forgot you were married. Tell those judges *that* when they ask." He shot me a look and his eyes reflected his hurt. "Maybe you should compete in the *Miss Pageant*." He turned and took one step to leave.

"Tom, Friday at three is the only day and time Dusty Joe has available. He's all booked up for months, and he works by referrals only. I'm not canceling." I threw my towel in the corner.

"And, if you believe that, you are gullible." He worked the muscles in his jaw.

My eyes watered and my throat tightened. "I'm not dumb, Tom. You don't get it. You don't understand. I thought you did, but obviously you don't." I tried to catch my breath and not cry.

"I can't wait until this pageant is over. It's ruining our lives." Tom slammed the office door.

I stood unable to move.

If only he understood why this pageant is more important to me than a birthday dinner.

Soon after the argument, I heard the sound of the lawn mower. I knew Tom was really upset. He always mowed the grass when he wanted to check out of reality for an hour.

Later that evening, I put the kids to bed and allowed enough time for both our emotions to simmer down. I cautiously approached Tom in the living room and cuddled up next to him on the couch. We sat silent. He let out a deep sigh before he placed his strong arm around my shoulders.

"I'm sorry, Tom. I should have asked you first about Friday. I was so excited, I forgot about celebrating my birthday."

He tilted his head and met my eyes. "It's all right, Lu. I'm starting to realize this is our new life, until this pageant is over. I'm trying to adjust. I will, I promise, but afterwards I get my old Lu back, right?" An easy grin played on his lips.

I looked at Tom, but didn't say anything. I didn't know if I wanted the old Lucy back. I liked the new Lucy, who was sprouting from the dirt and blossoming. With tender care, she would soon be in full bloom.

"I thought about it," Tom said. "We can do both. I'll drive you to the studio on Friday. When you're done, we should still have enough time to make it to your birthday dinner."

"Thank you. I knew you would make it work. Only two weeks left until my pageant workshop." I held up two fingers. "And in four weeks it's pageant night. "I added two more. "The big day," I deepened my voice, "The last hurrah. The make-it-or-break-it day."

Tom laughed and let his head fall back against the couch. After a thoughtful moment, he turned, took hold of my shoulders, and looked straight into my eyes. "I can't wait. I get you back then, right?" His breath touched my cheek. He ran his fingers through my curls while he waited for my answer.

"Yes, I'll be back, I promise. Unless..." My voice held a hint of humor. "I win."

His words were soft and low. "Remember Lu, no matter what happens, you are a queen to me. My queen."

But there was a look in Tom's eye, which made me think he secretly hoped I would lose.

~

It was almost three o'clock when Tom drove in and parked on the road where Dusty Joe's photo studio was located. There wasn't a car or person or cat in sight.

"You said three o'clock, right?" Tom checked the clock on the dashboard.

"This is the place, isn't it?" I asked.

"Looks like Dusty Joe is busting at the seams with business." Tom patted my knee. "That's why he works by referral only."

"Oh, Tom. Just because the street is empty doesn't mean anything." I released the latch on the door handle then loaded my arms with various outfits. "Are you going to mind waiting out here?" I kicked the passenger door open.

"It's no big deal. Go, have fun."

I walked around the SUV and Tom rolled down his window. "I'm fine. You go, you smile big and you be beautiful. I'll read the sports section. I'll take a nap." Tom slouched down in his seat. "I'll people watch." He looked at me from the corner of his eye.

"Like there are so many people around." I took a panoramic glance at the empty sidewalks. "I'll try to hurry so we're not late for dinner." I leaned through the window and gave him a quick kiss. "I smell rain." Dark clouds moved toward us.

"Don't worry. Take your time, relax, and look pretty for the camera. I'm totally fine." Tom snapped open the sports section of the newspaper.

I took a couple of steps backward, blew Tom a kiss, and then rushed to the photographer's front door. A large sign read, *Dusty Joe Westbrook's Photography at its Finest.* Under the headline, in script, it read, *'Look like a winner.'* A pageant crown looped around the 'L' in the word *look.* I paused and looked at my husband. He seemed content, his full attention on the newspaper. My heart softened. He may not understand the pageant world, but he was there for me.

After taking a deep breath I entered the studio. Three steps in I stopped to soak in the alternate universe I stumbled into.

A white Maltese rested in an argyle purple and black doggy bed, underneath a wooden plaque that read, "Molly." She lifted her head to check me out, sniffed three times then lowered herself back onto the doggie bed, seemingly unimpressed.

There wasn't anyone to be seen in the studio, but Dusty Joe already had his camera, spotlights, and equipment set up. My feet vibrated, and a sensation traveled up my legs from the loud music, streaming from his built-in stereo system. I recognized the song, "Jessie's Girl," from the 1980s. I pushed my glasses up and bounced to the beat of Rick Springfield.

A wall to the left was ghetto-style, adorned with multi-colored graffiti and metal bars, which formed the background. A metal crate was used as a prop and a large industrial fan faced the set. It looked cool and hip. A good backdrop for Dusty Joe's teenage clients.

The other side of the room was painted hot pink. Feathered boas were scattered on the floor and draped over the top of the high-back chairs. A pink feather floated toward the floor. I was tempted to run and catch it. A gaudy chandelier and an oversized mirror, like one found in theater dressing rooms, hung from the ceiling.

I should bring Suzy here for pictures. She would go crazy in the princess set.

The camera was set up and focused on the stark-white back wall. A yellow-taped X marked the floor, where I assumed I would pose for my photos.

"Hellooo gorgeous." Dusty Joe walked with purpose as he approached me. "You must be Lucy. Courtney told me all about you." He gave me a snappy hug as if we were long-time friends.

"Nice to meet you." I put my purse on the floor.

"I don't want you to worry about a thing." Dusty Joe showcased his bleached, straight teeth from his perfect tanned face with a smile

New clothes, a pageant coach, high-heel lessons, and now a professional photographer. Surreal. The studio brought back a memory of when I was a little girl who dreamed of becoming a princess. I was overwhelmed, but at the same time, Dusty Joe made me feel safe, secure, and special. I had no choice but to trust him with this all-important photo shoot. The program book would be in the hands of the judges, even before the first portion of competition, the interview. Dusty Joe held an important part of my victory in his hands.

He turned the music down a few decibels and spoke rapidly as he fidgeted with the equipment. "I know a pageant headshot is the first impression the judges will see of you." He adjusted the settings on his camera.

While he was busy, I sized him up. About five-foot ten, lean, and in his early thirties. He wore spotless, shiny, black Gucci shoes, posh jeans and a striped pink and sky blue button-down shirt, with the top three buttons undone. He knew fashion better than I did. With his thick dark hair, black-rimmed glasses, and square jaw, he was handsome.

The more he projected energy, confidence, and fun the more nervous I became. I was out of my element, and definitely out of style. Boy, did he have his work cut out for him making my pictures look glamorous.

"Your photo will be a valuable tool. It needs to convince the judges you are the lady to crown." He looked at me for a long second. "I'll take a couple of different shots, and send them to my girl, Courtney. The two of you can decide which photo you like best." He was quick on his feet as he darted back and forth adjusting the spotlights, rearranging the many cords, and moving the stool until it was in the perfect position.

"A head shot with direct eye contact is what we want. Nothing cutesy or creative. We don't want you looking over your shoulder or holding a rose. And no full-body photos."

"Okay," was all I could say before I put my extra carefully folded clothes on a stool nearby. I didn't want to distract him. I wanted to hear every word Dusty Joe said. I needed all of the instructions, directions, and tips.

He circled me, studying my hairstyle, and lightly touched my hair. "Is this how you are going to wear your strawberry hair during the pageant?"

"I think so." I bit my lip.

He removed my glasses and laid them on top of my clothes. The gesture made me feel comfortable, like we'd known each other forever. "Your photo needs to match exactly with the way the judges will see you during pageant weekend. No surprises. If we do this right, they will feel as if they already know you."

I barely managed to say, "I understand." I wanted to throw my arms around him in gratitude and tell him he was the greatest.

"My goal today is to capture a classic and timeless headshot. Not only do I want you to win the pageant, but I want you to win 'Mrs. Photogenic.'" Dusty Joe winked at me. "The winning photograph will accent your best features. The judges will recognize you as the lady with the beautiful strawberry blonde hair who is elegant and confident."

With Dusty Joe's help, it didn't take long to get comfortable with the bright lights and the clicking of the camera in my face.

Sooner than I expected, he said, "It's a wrap."

I let out a deep breath.

"Lucy, I'm not a judge, but it's my brilliant opinion that you have the whole package, girlfriend. The winning package. Good luck to you."

"Thank you, Dusty Joe." I treasured his words, *winning package,* like precious gold.

"I'll be rooting for you on pageant night."

"You're going to be there?"

"Girlfriend," He brushed his hand like he was swatting at a pesky fly. "Don't be silly, of course I will be there. Besides, I'm the pageant's official photographer."

Oh, a professional photographer, I hadn't realized.

"I appreciate the time you spent with me this afternoon." I wrote a check to him for the photo shoot.

The front door jangled, and I looked up. Molly with painted red toenails gave out a happy yelp.

A tall man ran his hand through his wind-blown, strikingly gorgeous, feathered blonde hair, walked over, and scooped her up. I tried not to stare. He wore a tight, white, muscle tank top tucked into his faded denim jeans, with a physique that reminded me of *Fabio.*

"It's wet out there." He looked straight at me and held my gaze.

I dropped my head embarrassed that he caught me gawking and finished signing my name on the check. "It's raining?" I ripped out the check and stole another look at this handsome man who now was letting Molly lick his chiseled cheekbones.

"It just started. The roads could be slippery with oil."

"Thanks for the warning." I handed the check to Dusty Joe, gathered my things, and headed toward the front door. The man smiled at me when I walked past him. Closing the door behind me, I looked one more time through the glass door. Dusty Joe greeted him with a long embrace and a kiss.

Excited about the past hour I hustled to our vehicle, opened the car door and threw my purse and wardrobe into the back seat.

"All done?" Tom mumbled and scooted up.

"All done."

"That was fast. Ready for your birthday dinner?"

"Yeah, I'm starved. Let's go."

~TWELVE~
Crunch

Sunbeams streamed through the raindrops, hitting the windshield. *I love liquid sun.* I closed my eyes, listened to the sound of the patter from the drops and relaxed.

Tom nudged me. "Don't doze off. We're going to be at the restaurant any minute."

A cute sports car zipped around us and snagged my attention.

"Looks like we're not driving fast enough," Tom turned his wipers up a speed. I caught a glimpse of the silver 350Z Nissan. It strutted personalized license plates that read, NAW T.

"I have a great idea, Tom." I sat up straighter. "After I win this pageant, maybe we can buy personalized license plates for me."

He turned the radio dial down. "Whoa, Lu. You haven't won yet."

Caught. I proclaimed my victory too soon.

Don't get ahead of yourself." Tom kept his eyes on the road. "Just because a car zooms by us with personalized plates doesn't mean you need them too."

"Zoom, zoom, and a boom, boom," I sang and snapped my fingers trying to cover my embarrassment. "It could say 'Mrs. Oregon' or 'Go Girl' or how about 'Winner?'" I ignored Tom's reluctance.

"Lucy, win or lose, I'll buy you license plates that say, 'My Queen.'" He looked at me and winked.

I reached down and turned the radio volume back up. When I looked up, I saw a splash of silver. Everything happened so fast. "Tom! Look out!" I braced myself against the dashboard. The tires screeched. A loud crunch, a wave of heat, and the smell of burnt rubber assaulted us. The airbag inflated and smacked me in the face. A dull ache rolled through my body.

People stopped on the side of the road with looks of shock and horror. Things happened in slow motion. Onlookers stared and rocked on their heels while on their cell phones.

My eyelids were heavy. I wanted to sleep. I closed my eyes.

"Lucy? Lucy? Are you okay? Honey. Lucy." It took me a moment to register his voice. "Lucy, look at me, Honey. Can you turn your head toward me?"

My throat felt dry. I couldn't find my voice. I sat motionless.

"Lucy." Panic vibrated in Tom's voice.

I had to say something to assure him I was okay. "What happened?" I struggled to open my eyes.

"We hit the silver car."

"Are they okay?"

"I don't know. Are you okay?"

"I think so." I touched my nose and mouth and looked at my hand. I didn't see any blood, but my lip felt big and getting bigger. I flipped down the visor and looked in the mirror. Deep purple moons adorned both eyes.

"Will you be okay while I find out about the other people in the car?"

"Uh-huh, I'm fine."

"Sit up. I don't want you to fall asleep," he said.

"Okay."

"Looks like the air-bag kissed you hard. I'm sorry, Lu." He looked at me closely.

Tom went to check on the person driving the sports car and I looked out the windshield. Tom was bent over the driver side window, not moving, not even talking. Groggily, I turned my head to the right to where other people were standing with their cell phones out. They too were motionless, not even talking. Everything outside of our car seemed frozen in time. Finally Tom walked back to our vehicle. He swiped droplets of rainwater from his forehead.

"There is only one lady, the driver and the EMTs think she might have whiplash. Other than that, she's fine, but her car is totaled." Tom looked pale. "Do you want the EMTs to check on you, Lucy?"

"No, I'm fine. I hope she'll be okay. How much damage to our car?"

"The bumper's smashed in, but nothing I can't fix." More sirens approached. Tom stepped out of our SUV again to take care of the police report and insurance information.

Strangers stopped and directed traffic around the crash scene.

Tom ran his trembling fingers through his wet hair. He stood next to the driver, a young girl, trying to comfort her, as she explained her side of the story to the officer. She waved her hands wildly and pointed her finger at our car. The tow truck arrived and secured the silver car with the now dented personalized license plates.

The girl's shoulders shook, and she sobbed as if she had just lost her best friend.

I climbed out to join them. Between sobs and gasping for air, she explained, "My car was a college graduation gift from my dad. He is going to be hopping mad and I'm sure he won't buy me another one."

"I like your license plates," I said.

Tom whipped his head toward me and glared.

I must have hit my head pretty hard to say something like that.

He then put his arm around the stranger's shoulder, comforting her. As she calmed down, Tom reached for his cell phone and punched the buttons.

"Are you calling our insurance agent?" I asked.

"No, your mom, I need to tell her we'll be late for your birthday dinner."

Even in a crisis, he thinks of everything.

I hesitated. "We're still going out to eat? Tom, really, we don't have to. We can just go home. My parents will understand."

"There's nothing more we can do tonight. We might as well keep our dinner plans. Besides, it's your birthday, remember? It'll be better than just sitting at home staring at the TV and thinking about the wreck. Plus, I'm hungry."

I nodded in shock, too numb to object. After all of the legal reports were completed and the sports car towed away, we left the scene in silence and drove in the now dented SUV in the direction of the restaurant.

Fifteen minutes later, we arrived at Joey's Pizzeria. I stepped out of the car my legs wobbled and my arms were weak. Tom took my hand and we entered the familiar restaurant. The hostess directed us to the banquet room at the back of the building.

I heard familiar voices. "Uh Tom, did you invite everyone?" I tugged on his arm.

"Shhh," he gave an eager grin.

"Is this a birthday party? *Myyy* birthday party?"

We entered the large banquet room, and there were Selena, Colleen, Sandra, Julie and their husbands. "The whole Gang is here." Tears pooled in my eyes, and I laughed and cried at the same time, comforted by our friends.

Tom put his arm around me. Everyone was quiet. Then Julie started singing "Happy Birthday" and the rest of the Gang joined in. We found our seats while everyone visited. We studied the menu and gave the waitress our order. I thanked Tom and the Gang for the nice surprise.

While we waited for our pizza, Tom told the group every detail about hitting the silver car. He finished telling the dramatic story to The Gang just as Claudia arrived with our three kids. I quickly rushed to them, giving each one a huge hug. Even seeing Claudia there, visiting among our friends, sent a current of gratitude through my body for family and relationships.

Thank you God, Claudia had the kids and they weren't in the SUV with us.

"Mommy, you have raccoon eyes," Suzy told me.

I returned her smile through my swollen lips.

Claudia came over and hugged me. "Everything will be alright."

It didn't take long for the pizza and sodas to arrive. As the night went on, my emotions settled. Jake and Adam asked Grandpa for quarters to play video games, and Suzy climbed on his lap. The room filled with laughter and chatter. In a short time the round, metal pizza trays, which had been filled with Pepperoni and Hawaiian style pizza, were empty.

Mom left the banquet room and came back in carrying a homemade birthday cake with my favorite fluffy, white frosting and the number thirty-three placed on top.

"Time for cake." Tom stood and passed out paper plates.

I pointed to the cake, "Did you think I forgot how old I am, Mom?" I laughed, then winced from the pain in my lip.

Selena cleared the center of the table so Mom could set the cake down.

Julie pulled a gift from underneath her chair. "Here." She handed me a large beautifully wrapped box with a big bow. "This is from the whole Gang."

"You guys…" My face flushed. "You didn't have to do that. But I'm glad you did."

Everyone laughed.

I found my glasses, unwrapped the box and lifted the lid. There was a beautiful black and white Jackie Kennedy look-alike dress.

"We thought you could wear the outfit to pageant weekend," Selena said.

My eyes watered and I blinked quickly. I was overly emotional because of everything that happened today. My friends were proving to be supportive throughout these months of obsession. It was impossible to convey my appreciation. "Thank you, I love it. I will definitely wear it, and I have the perfect shoes to match, if my coach approves." I folded the dress and placed it back inside the box.

Julie handed her gift to me and I opened it.

"Thanks, Jules. Vera Wang cologne. My favorite." I stepped around the chair and gave her a hug.

"I know. I want you to wear it on pageant night for good luck."

Claudia stepped in and handed her gift to me.

"Thank you, this must be a book." I ripped off the wrapping paper. "I love to lose myself in a good book." I held the book high, so everyone could see the title. *How to Become Organized and Structured in Life.*

Of course, it would be a self-help book.

"I thought it would come in handy while you're adding another new project to your plate." Claudia struggled to explain her gift, as if trying to blend in with the theme of the party.

"I'll read it, Claudia. If I can stay organized enough to find it."

Selena and Colleen went together and bought me a gift certificate to my favorite spa for acrylic nails and a pedicure. Sandra bought me a journal to write down my pageant experience. My friends and family were the best.

Mom handed me a small, beautifully wrapped gift.

I slowly unwrapped and opened the small box. Inside was a pearl necklace.

"It was your grandmother's necklace. Now, I want you to have it." Mom's voice was soft.

I lifted the delicate, authentic strand of pearls from the box.

My friends gasped, followed with a chorus of oohs and aahs.

"Oh, Mom! Grandma's pearl necklace." My hand covered my heart.

"I thought you could wear it on pageant day with your interview suit. I know we haven't found the perfect suit yet, but we will."

"It's beautiful." I hugged her and whispered, "Thank you."

Tom stood, cleared his throat, and announced, "It's my turn." He took an envelope from his inside coat pocket.

Everyone quieted. Ron scooted to the edge of his seat and Colleen's eyes sparkled like they anticipated something big.

"Ah, Tom, what's this?" I accepted the envelope.

"My birthday gift to you. This is why I wasn't letting the car accident ruin my, I mean your, big day... and, the Gang is included, too. You'll know what I mean. Open it." He stood close to watch me.

All of our friends' eyes were on me, waiting. It was obvious they knew what was in the envelope.

"But, you already bought me a treadmill for my birthday," I sweetly protested.

"Open the envelope." Tom winked. "That treadmill isn't your only present."

I tore into the envelope and in my hand lay two tickets for a cruise to the Caribbean. "A cruise, a cruise! Wow, Tom." My heart raced. "Now I understand why it was so important for us to make it here today."

I sneaked a look at the dates on the tickets to see if it would interrupt my pageant or my pageant preparations. The cruise dates would fit nicely into my schedule.

I lifted my head to see my friends' reactions. Each one had their hand in the air holding a cruise ticket. Goose bumps quickly progressed up my body. "What? We're *all* going together?" I laughed out loud. My friends clapped and I did a little hop. I made my way around the table and hugged each one.

Now, it all made sense. This is why Tom was concerned about the pageant expenses.

I gave Tom a kiss and touched my sore lip again.

"Claudia has another gift, too," Tom announced in a way to make sure she didn't feel left out. "She agreed to watch the kids while we bask in the sun and have fun." He smiled at her.

"I'm delighted," Claudia added.

"Thank you everyone. I mean it. Thank you very much. I'm looking forward to going away with all of you."

We stayed and talked about the itinerary, cruise wear and getting a tan for our vacation before leaving the restaurant. Tom and my dad gathered my gifts and Mom collected the bows to save for another day.

On the way home, I didn't stop chattering to Tom and the kids about what a wonderful day it turned out to be after all, despite the car accident. I thanked Tom again…and continued to thank him late into the night.

~THIRTEEN~
Round and Round

While running on the treadmill, I mentally cheered as the calorie counter canceled out the pizza and birthday cake. Now, I had doubled my motivation to lose weight. The pageant and the upcoming cruise.

I slowed down the treadmill, rubbed the back of my neck and rolled my shoulders, working out kinks and sore muscles sustained from the accident the night before. I was proud of myself for getting on the treadmill every day, but especially today. Fifteen pounds lighter my stamina had improved, now able to accomplish four miles, five times a week.

To help me stay focused, I quoted my mantra out loud, "A winner never quits," matching each word to the sound of my foot hitting the fast-moving belt.

The red light on the office answering machine kept blinking. It drove me crazy but I ignored it as I huffed and puffed through my last few minutes. Finally I turned off the treadmill and hit 'play' in the now quiet room.

"Hi, Lucy. This is Courtney. For our next session, please meet me at the Springfield School District in the main office at the usual time. Hope all is going well, and you're studying the fifty mock questions. See you on Tuesday."

Strange. Why did Courtney want to hold a session at the school?

~

Tuesday at 3:15, Mom and I stood outside the school breezeway waiting for Courtney to show up. We had no idea where we were supposed to go or what we were doing.

Yellow school buses full of children lined the parking lot waiting for their departure. Without thinking, I hummed the children's song *The Wheels on the Bus*. Ugh, this little ditty would be stuck in my head all day.

"I don't get it, Mom. Why do you think Courtney wanted to coach me here?" I searched my purse for some chap stick.

"Knowing Courtney, she has a good reason. She has good reasons for everything. And, there she is." Mom waved.

Courtney, dressed in a black pencil skirt and a sky blue, buttoned down, collared shirt, greeted us with a beautiful confident smile. "Hi, Lucy. Hi, Lucinda. Curious aren't you?"

Courtney led us down the empty school hall to the teachers' break room. Inside were three desks several feet apart, with a chair on both sides.

In the corner was a trio holding what looked like a friendly conversation. Courtney walked up to a gentleman with a goatee wearing a tweed jacket. "Lucy, may I present Mr. Baker, the school principle. He smiled at me as I shook his hand. With a smooth hand motion Courtney introduced a slender, honey blonde woman. "This is Ms. Larson, the ninth grade English teacher."

I forced myself not to think back to my high school years. The pain I experienced every day when I was made to leave English, in the middle of class, for the Title One Special Ed, flushed my face.

Courtney ended the introductions with a young student, who conducted herself with poise and class. "And this is Becky, one of the Journalism students. She has competed in several teen pageants. They're good friends of mine, who are always kind enough to help me with my pageant clients."

A poke from my mom reminded me of my manners and I introduced her to the trio. "This is my mom, Lucinda."

"Today, we are going to prepare you for your individual private interviews." Courtney glided across the room. "On pageant day, you'll meet five to seven judges, one at a time. Interviews are where pageants are won…or lost."

I shifted my weight and bit my lower lip.

"A judge forms an opinion about you in the first eight seconds of meeting you. So, even your walk into the interview room is extremely important. You must walk with grace, energy, and confidence. Begin with a smile and make eye contact with the judge immediately. Greet each one with enthusiasm. If you have to, drink an espresso before your interview to keep your energy up." She turned toward me. "And don't bite your lower lip."

Mom scribbled notes so I could simply let the instructions sink in. Later I'd review, study, and memorize everything that Courtney said.

"When you sit, slide on the chair gracefully, cross your legs at the ankles, not at the knee. Sit erect, with poise. Do not slouch or lean back in your chair." Courtney lowered herself into the chair and showed me how it was done. "I like to place my right palm in my left palm, resting on my lap, facing up. This conveys a message that 'I'm an open book and approachable.'" Courtney demonstrated the hand position. "Also, this prevents you from clenching your fists, pointing your finger, or twisting your ring." She paused. "Lucy, this private interview is the time to capture the judge's interest. You need to reveal your personality, intelligence and confidence. No lackluster performance. You must stand out, so the judges will look for you during the other areas of competition"

I looked at Courtney's three friends and stifled a chuckle. Each one had their elbow on their desk, with their chin resting in the palm of their hand. It was an odd sight.

They obviously had heard this speech before and could probably recite it word for word.

"You need to energize a dull interview by weaving in a sense of humor. The judges will remember a good laugh, and you will seem much more relaxed. The judges are just as nervous as you are, so a little levity helps."

I shifted back and forth and wiped my clammy hands on my skirt.

Courtney organized her three friends behind the desks with sheets of typed questions in front of them. "Okay, Lucy, I have a stopwatch here. Let's begin at Mr. Baker's desk. He will ask you a few questions. Your allotted time goes by quickly and a judge may only ask you three or four questions. Sometimes a judge may ask you only one question and stay with that same topic the whole five minutes. If this happens, you need the skill to weave in the key points about yourself you want the judge to know. You must control the interview without the interviewer realizing it. Understand?"

I nodded but inwardly controlling a conversation with complete strangers scared me.

"Okay, let's move on. After four minutes and thirty seconds, I will ring this bell—a thirty second warning bell." She picked up the bell and rang it. "Take that last thirty seconds to make your closing remarks. Then you will stand up with ease and shift to the next judge."

I mentally patted myself on the back for taking the time to practice answering Courtney's fifty mock questions while on my treadmill. "Okay, this should be fun." I smiled with assurance. *I could do this.*

After an hour of questions and answers, Courtney gave me a brief hug. *I must have done a good job.* I hoped the real judges on pageant night were as nice as this trio.

"You would be surprised how many women get tongue-tied with the easiest questions like, 'Why did you enter this pageant?' Or be stumped by a question about what they wrote in their bio for the judges. I'm glad to see you have your bio memorized. One of my favorite questions is, 'What is your favorite book and author?' Do you have one?" Courtney gave me a look that said she wasn't sure I could answer quickly enough.

"My favorite book is *'Yes, Yes Living in a No, No World'*, written by Neil Eskelin," I said with an I-know-my-bio smile.

"Nice job, Lucy. How about this question?" Courtney looked up, paused for a second, as if trying to surprise me with a difficult question, "What person do you admire most, and why?"

Even with all my hard work, I drew a blank. I couldn't think of a person, not even one.

"Don't make it harder than it is. Work on knowing the answer to that question. It should be easy. Everyone admires someone for something."

I nodded, glad I had answered one of her questions, but disappointed the last one befuddled me. I needed to practice the answers several times a day to break the nerve barrier.

"A lot of the interview technique is charisma, an art you can learn. It helps if you like being with people. Use the power of personality and sparkle." Courtney thanked her three friends, and I followed suit.

"I think I'm going to make a special point to come watch this year's pageant," the principal told me with a big grin. "Courtney has invited me to attend a pageant for years. This just may be the year." He winked at me.

"That would be wonderful. I need as many people in my spectator section as I can get." I smiled back at him, and then flashed a gentle smile toward Ms. Lawson and Becky. They also assured me they would be there on my big night to cheer me on.

As we walked out, Courtney said, "Remember, there are no right or wrong answers to any of the questions. The answers are just your opinions on topics, coupled with how well you deliver them.

In the parking lot, Courtney had one last piece of advice. "On pageant weekend, you will be sequestered from the public. You'll receive your pageant program book from headquarters. While you are in your hotel room, make sure you read and memorize the judge's names, accomplishments, beliefs and passions. All of this information will be in the program book. You do not want to accidentally offend a judge by insulting their beliefs during private interviews." She winked.

"Good advice," I said, glad once more to have hired Courtney.

"Be prepared. If you start talking too much you'll sound like your thoughts are disorganized. Don't ramble. Try to answer the question the judge asks without repeating the questions back. This only takes up precious time and the judges can see right through it. They will know you are stalling to get your thoughts organized. This will only irritate them. If you need time to collect your thoughts, simply pause then answer them directly, straight to the point. Speak precisely."

By now, we had arrived at Courtney's car. "If a judge asks you what your worst quality is, make sure you put a positive spin on it. For example, a fault could be that you are a workaholic. The positive spin to being a workaholic is determination, dedication and the will to complete the job."

"I understand. Take my weak point and turn it into a strength."

"Your goal is to create a positive impression. If you don't know an answer just admit it to the judges. Don't try to make something up. It could backfire. However, if it calls for your opinion, you'd better have an answer. The judges admire a woman who is not afraid to have an opinion, even an unpopular one." Courtney opened her car door. "And Lucy, if you walk out feeling you had a tough interview, consider it a compliment. Judges are thrilled when they meet someone who is knowledgeable and confident, someone who can answer difficult questions."

I gave Courtney a big hug. "Thank you again, Courtney, for sharing all of your pageant secrets with me."

The sky was streaked yellow and red when I arrived home after dropping off Mom. I entered the living room to see Tom, Jake, and Suzy watching Eye-Spy our favorite reality television show. "Sorry, it's late," I heel kicked the door closed. "Where's Adam?" I dropped my purse in the hall closet, along with my jacket.

Tom paused the program and turned toward me. "He's in his room. He's upset." Tom shrugged. "I thought I would wait until you got home before I asked him for a fifth time what was wrong." Tom turned back toward the television and pushed 'play' on the remote.

Instantly, my mood changed from being excited to share with Tom what I learned in the series of mock interviews to disappointment, I just stood there.

Adam crossed in front of the television. With lips tightened and eyes narrowed he plopped down on the couch and folded his arms.

"Hi, Adam." He refused to glance in my direction.

I stared at him, encouraging him to look at me. His posture seemed to indicate anger. I struggled to think of a reason but came up empty.

"What's wrong?" Tom directed his question to Adam.

"Nothin'."

"Did you get into trouble with your teacher?" I moved in front of Adam to read his expression.

Adam shook his head.

"Did someone say something to you at school?" Tom turned the television off while he waited for an answer.

Adam kept his head down and stared at his hands.

Struggling to be patient, I gritted my teeth waiting for Adam's answer.

"I know. I know what's wrong," Jake answered for Adam.

"Shut up, Jake!" Adam clenched his fists.

Tom and I both looked at Jake and then back at Adam. Tom held up a hand. "Adam, just tell us what's wrong. Did you do something? We won't be mad at you."

"Why were you at my school today?" Adam blurted his question. He glanced around the room, still refusing to look at me.

"You're asking me?" I placed my hand on my chest.

"Yeah, I saw you from the school bus window. Why were you at *my* school?"

"It has nothing to do with you, Honey. Do you think the principal called me?"

I didn't think he even noticed I was at his school. Tom raised his eyebrows at me, as if to say *this is all your fault.* I shook my head at him. Why that upset Adam, I had no idea.

"I know it's not about me. It's about you!" Red blotches crept up Adam's neck.

"Me?" I put my hand on my forehead. "What do I have to do with anything?"

Tom's head went back and forth between us like he was witnessing a ping-pong match.

Jake jumped in, eager to let us know why Adam was mad. "All of the boys on the school bus were making nasty comments about you to Adam."

I looked at Tom, and then to Jake, and back to Adam.

Adam glared. "I said shut up, Jake, or I'll punch you."

Jake dashed for his bedroom. Yelling over his shoulder the whole way, "A kid on the bus said really loud, 'Adam, your mom is *hot*,' and stuff I can't repeat. Another kid asked if you were his older sister." The door slammed shut and the lock clicked.

"I hope you told him to shut up or else." Tom jumped into the conversation and probed Adam for a reply.

"Tom, stop it. It isn't Adam's responsibility to stick up for me," I interrupted. "Let's not make this worse than it is."

"Adam, don't let them talk about your mom like that," Tom demanded.

"I didn't say anything, okay! It's embarrassing enough!" Adam bounced off the sofa. "Now, you're going to enter a stupid beauty pageant. It'll just get worse." he stormed out of the living room and seconds later we heard his bedroom door slam shut.

That explained why he was upset. I turned my attention to Tom, my voice soft. "You can't ask him to defend me."

"Sure I can. He shouldn't let those kids say those kinds of things about you."

"He has enough pressures in school. It's hard enough to get along with kids. He doesn't need you pressuring him to make the boys stop saying things about me. He wants to fit in."

"If anyone ever said those things about *my* mom, I would have shoved a pencil up his nose." Tom remained adamant.

"That was twenty years ago, Tom. Things are different now. Those boys could retaliate with punches. He could be kicked out of school. Besides, Adam is only ten, not sixteen. The boys on the bus who said those things were probably a lot older than he is. He doesn't need to fight my battles. Drop it Tom. I don't want this to come between Adam and me. He already won't be seen with me. He makes me walk ten yards away from him."

"Mom, I like it that you're pretty." Suzy snuggled closer to me.

"All of my friends think I'm cool, because you don't look old enough to be my mom." Jake hugged me from the other side.

"Ah, thanks, guys." Their comments eased some of the pain, but my heart still ached for Adam.

I waited until the house quieted down before I padded to Adam's room. I cracked open the door and saw him lying on his bed, one arm under his pillow and the other covering his face. I heard his shallow breathing and knew he was asleep. For a long time I stood in his doorway before I tiptoed to his bed. I unfolded the crocheted blanket that Grandma Lucinda made for him last Christmas and spread it over him.

Adam turned his head, opened his eyes halfway, and looked at me.

"I'm sorry, sweetheart. I know I embarrassed you at school today." I ran my fingers through his hair.

"It's okay, Mom." Adam turned his head back toward the wall.

"Honey, I want you to be proud of me not embarrassed of me. Those boys didn't mean to hurt your feelings." I continued stroking his hair.

In the darkened room, Claudia's words rushed into my mind, *Why are you putting Tom and the kids through a ridiculous beauty pageant? What are you teaching Suzy about beauty and vanity?* She accused me of being empty inside. I didn't have the courage to tell her the *real* reasons I was competing. I couldn't bring myself to tell her that under all the extra weight, lack of fashion sense, and low self-esteem, I wanted to prove I was beautiful. I deserved to be on stage, just as much as any other woman. God made me special too, and He wanted me to shine in life. More important than anything else, I wanted Tom to be proud of me once again. I shook off Claudia's taunting remarks, and kissed Adam on the cheek.

"I'm sorry, Adam." I whispered.

~FOURTEEN~
Dates

I stepped off the treadmill after a forty-minute workout, reenergized and invigorated. Four weeks left to reach my goal weight for pageant night. I wrapped a towel around my neck and cruised toward the kitchen wearing my hot pink sports bra and black shorts. The aroma of coffee guided my way.

Tom looked handsome, dressed in a business suit with his tie loose, standing in front of the refrigerator. With his hand to his forehead he stared at the calendar, his other hand pressed against the door, as if he needed something more to hold him up.

"You look like you just lost your best friend." I bounced into the kitchen and reached for my favorite coffee mug.

"I think I did." Tom stared at me. "Have you seen this calendar? You're going to be gone somewhere every single day."

I avoided eye contact with him, staring at my mug as if it was the first time I'd seen it. "Of course I saw the calendar. I'm the one who wrote on it every single day, silly." I set my mug on the kitchen counter and dumped coffee into it. I didn't like the direction these questions were headed. I took a step around Tom, opened the refrigerator, and grabbed the carton of cream, then poured it into my concoction of sugar and coffee. Hopefully, he would notice how marvelous I looked in my workout shorts, and see how my hard work was paying dividends. I thought I deserved a compliment instead of a lecture.

"Who's going to take care of the kids while you're gallivanting around town, playing dress up and spending money?" Tom turned his attention back to the calendar on the refrigerator. He released a slow breath and pointed at the two-inch square that had Wednesday circled in red, the day Courtney and I were scheduled to go to the big city to shop for a new interview suit and evening gown.

"Monday, speaking engagement. Tuesday, coaching. Wednesday, shopping. Thursday, tanning, hair and nails. Lucy, this never ends!" Tom pointed and tapped his finger on each square of the week. He pivoted toward me.

I needed to change the subject and distract him. I performed the bend and snap theory from *Legally Blonde*. I held my breath, waiting for his compliment about my weight loss and firmer body.

Instead, he pointed his finger at me. "You know, this family doesn't revolve around you. It's not all about Lucy."

"That's not fair, Tom Rupp, and you know it." My voice cracked. "I've done everything for this family for thirteen years! It has *never* been about me. So, let me have nine months, would you please? Get off my back!"

"Nine months? Nine months, yeah right. Nine months will lead to nine years. I don't see this ever ending."

"What? Do you own a crystal ball?" I knew I sounded sarcastic, but his fluctuating support had me whip-lashed.

"Once you start something, it never ends." He turned his back on me and walked out of the kitchen, tossing the last comment over his shoulder. "You're obsessed."

"What are you afraid of, Tom?" My question followed him.

"Losing you," he whispered right before he slammed the front door.

I couldn't move, like an anchor had pinned my legs to the floor. I didn't want to think about what he had said. *Losing you.* I shrugged. He didn't really mean it. I just wanted to go forward with my dreams, ideas, and plans.

I walked back to the refrigerator and flipped through the calendar, looking at all of my penciled entries. My heart sank, the seven days for the cruise were not blocked out, I groaned. Tom probably thought it wasn't important enough for me to write down the dates and I didn't appreciate his birthday gift.

I found a red pen and outlined the box around each day we would be away. I wanted him to know I hadn't forgotten we would be spending time together with The Gang. This time, I wouldn't be intimidated to go away with our friends. I smiled at the thought of relaxing in a hot tub. This time, I felt good about myself. This time, on the cruise, I would look great in a bathing suit. This time, I would fit in with the girls.

The way Tom left this morning bothered me more than I wanted to admit. He didn't understand why the pageant was important to me, why I was driven to win. My girlfriends would understand. I needed some girl talk and dialed Julie's number.

"I'm so tired of fighting," I told Julie on the telephone. I wore my hands-free headset while I moved around the house picking up children's books, toys and clothes that were scattered about.

"Uh-huh." Julie sounded bored.

"Seems like all we do lately is fight."

"I hope this pageant is worth it."

Guess I wasn't going to get any sympathy from my long-time friend. Add her to the list of people who don't understand.

"I need to go. I still have to jump in the shower and get ready for the day. Talk to ya soon." We exchanged goodbyes.

After I hung up, glad to be alone. I went to my bedroom, closed the door, and found my stash of chocolate hidden in the closet. I unwrapped a piece, popped it in my mouth, closed my eyes, and let it melt as I savored the taste.

Chocolate helped but I couldn't afford these calories. *What could I do?* I changed into the outfit my girlfriends bought for my birthday and looked at my reflection in the mirror.

That's what I needed. Finally the pretty, thin, confident Lucy was emerging from the past. The real Lucy

~FIFTEEN~
Workshop

The clock on my cell phone displayed 6:50am as I dialed my mom. "Sorry I woke you. I'm pulling into the hotel parking lot now. I wish you were here with me," I exhaled my disappointment into my phone.

"You don't need me there, Lucy. You'll be just fine, take notes like I do." She sounded fully awake now.

Mom had always been crazy about her notes.

"You're going to learn so much." She added.

"I know, Mom, but I'm nervous." I shifted into park and turned off the ignition, glancing at my image in the rear view mirror, hoping my chin remained free of monthly acne for seven more hours. "I'm meeting all of the other pageant women for the first time." I threw my keys into my purse. "I just wish you were here. That's all. You're my security blanket."

"Be sure to network and *make friends.*"

"Okay, I understand. I'll call you first thing tonight and tell you everything. Bye."

I entered the plush lobby of the Hilton, armed with my purse, a pen and notebook, mints, bottled water, hairbrush, and makeup tote, all in one large designer bag.

I tossed my coffee cup into the trash and walked straight to the lady's room for one last look-over before meeting the other contestants for the first time. I checked my hair and gave a nod of approval. I studied my makeup and reapplied the perfect shade of lipstick recommended by the cosmetologist, who came to Courtney's home for a one-on-one consultation. Of course I purchased everything the professional said I needed. My eyebrows were arched in just the right place. My teeth gleamed, thanks to my dentist's magic gel and light. My capris and matching shirt were wrinkle-free. With my back to the mirror I looked over my shoulder, one last time, to check my backside. I gave myself a satisfied smile.

Outside the lady's room, a sandwich board directed me to the Mrs. Oregon workshop. I followed bright red arrows down the carpeted hall to the banquet room and entered through the double doors.

A podium with a microphone was positioned at the front of the spacious room along with a large white board and several rows of chairs mirrored them. Around the room groups of three to four ladies chatted while waiting for the workshop to begin.

I glanced around trying not to look nervous, not sure I was in the right banquet room. I appeared to have wandered into a plastic surgery conference. The majority of women looked as though they were spokes models for breast enhancements, Botox and lip-injections, rather than participants in a pageant workshop. The ladies looked stunning. My throat tightened when I spotted the vinyl banner hanging on the back wall that confirmed I was at the right place.

All of the women wore the latest pageant hairstyles Courtney had told me I would see. Mrs. Bend, Oregon sported an elegant upswept hairdo. Mrs. Roseburg, wore her hair shorter and curled softly. A third of the women wore their hair in a long glamorous style, too sexy for a married ladies' pageant but that was my personal opinion.

I suppressed a laugh when I saw three women standing in a corner all wearing the exact same hairstyle. They wore long hair, teased at the crown, anchored back, classic, and beautiful. If I could get a barrette straight, I would wear that style.

Another lady's hair was styled into a sleek chignon. Of course there was one other lady in the room with my hairstyle. Just like Courtney coached, I had my hair chemically straightened, strawberry red shade enhanced and cut shoulder-length, softly curled under, with wispy bangs. It was a simple, easy-care look that hadn't been easy on my wallet. I stood out because of my red hair, which I liked, but I was concerned my style lacked the glamour needed for a pageant. I suspected the other women were checking me out too.

It didn't take me long to notice cliques had already formed. There I stood, alone.

Somebody, please tell me I'm not crazy for entering this pageant.

My musings came to an abrupt stop when the chatter quieted. Some stopped speaking mid-sentence. One by one, the ladies turned their heads toward the doorway. Silence. All eyes were on a woman who had just made a grand entrance... a beautiful, sexy woman projecting an aura which shouted, "Here I am!" She was tall. I guessed six feet with her high heels, and about a size two dress. Her obvious fake boobs led the way.

The whispering began. "Who's that?"

"Where did she come from?"

"Have you seen her before?" another lady asked her group of friends.

My eyes were like magnets, stuck on steel. *Please don't let her be a contestant. Please let her be on the pageant headquarters staff.* I begged the pageant gods.

The firecracker of a woman had platinum blonde hair, layered, not one strand out of place. She must have had three tall cans of hairspray in her designer bag. She reminded me of Farrah Fawcett in *Charlie's Angels.*

Her bold red, no-nonsense fitted suit with large rhinestones strategically placed on the lapels of the blazer was a showstopper. Her skirt stopped a well-calculated inch above her knees. Courtney would approve of her taupe four-inch high heels. Then I saw it. The sash over her chest displayed Mrs. Salem, Oregon. My heart sank like a ship's anchor and my breath caught in my throat. The pageant gods let me down. She was a contestant.

With her head held high and shoulders back, she glided past the different groups of ladies without acknowledging them. Not even a nod. She didn't smile. It was evident she was not here to make friends. She was here for one reason and one reason only—to win the Mrs. Oregon pageant.

I am competing against these women. They seemed so untouchable, unapproachable, unreal. I thought back to my treadmill and all the time I put in. All my coaching. I wanted to reach into my purse and bring out a piece of chocolate. I was clearly a rookie.

All eyes followed her to the front row where she took her seat. Her spine straight as a new pencil, she crossed her ankles and stared forward. Focused. Her presence commanded our attention. Heck, she owned the room.

I wanted to turn, run to my car clutching a chocolate bar, speed home and forget this whole crazy idea. More and more, it seemed I didn't belong. I wanted my mom.

The whispers continued in the room. "Maybe the judges will knock off points because she doesn't smile," said a tall brunette.

"If she did smile they would see right through it and know its fake," someone else chimed in.

"Like her boobs." The cattiness continued.

I chuckled at the last statement because it came from a contestant with bigger implants. In a weird way it comforted me to know that at least some of the other women had the same awful feelings.

The sound of high heels clicking came from behind me. Someone tapped my shoulder.

I turned to a lady with nickel-sized blue eyes and pretty blonde hair. She flashed a perfect pageant smile, revealing a mouth full of white veneers. All that was missing was the sound of a cymbal ting and a sparkle on the front tooth, just like the television toothpaste commercials. "Hi, I'm Stacey Smith." She swung her hair off her shoulder and pointed to her sash. "Mrs. Portland, Oregon." She held out her hand to shake mine. She spoke precisely and clearly, never breaking her smile.

"Nice to meet you I'm Lucy, Lucy Rupp. Mrs. Springfield." It was nice to have someone stand next to me, someone friendly to talk with. I wanted the other ladies in the room to notice that now I, too, had a friend.

Please don't walk away.

Her demeanor gave the impression she wasn't intimidated by anyone. Maybe she didn't see the woman who just made the grand entrance.

"Did you see the woman who just came in?" She tossed her hair with practiced skill and flashed her perfect, bright ivories again. Dollar signs poured from every pore. She pointed her chin and eyes at the tall Barbie-doll-like woman in the front row.

Yep, Stacey noticed her.

"Yes, I did. Who could miss her?" My tone was kind, yet careful. I stopped myself from rolling my eyes. I didn't want to give Stacey the impression I was catty, or worse, intimidated.

Do not let them see you sweat.

"What's her name?" I bit the inside of my cheek.

"I overheard some lady say her name is Mindy Storm." She whispered her name.

"She sure entered the room like a storm." The words flew out and I wished I had kept my big mouth shut.

"This is her first pageant, so we don't have anything to worry about."

"Oh?' I raised my eyebrows. *First pageant?*

Stacey explained, "Usually, first year girls *do not* win." She raised and tilted her chin in the air, sniffed once to emphasize she wasn't worried.

"First year girls?"

I'm a first time girl.

"The first time a woman enters a pageant, she rarely wins."

"Really?" *I'd never heard that before.* I found it hard to believe women actually went through this process more than once. "Have you entered before?" My eyes widened, hoping she would let me in on a big secret.

"Yes, this is my third time." Stacey waved three fingers in the air.

I thought I was going to blow over. These women, knowing what they were in for, would put themselves through this again.

"I figure next year is *my* year to win. My pageant coach has me on a four-year plan." Stacey popped up another finger to equal four. Her fingernails were perfectly enhanced with acrylic.

I couldn't imagine entering a pageant and not expecting to win. I planned on winning. "Four-year plan?" I wrinkled my nose.

"You know, you enter the first year to see if it's an experience you enjoy. If you do, then the second year you compete, and hope you are in the top ten. The third year, you want to make the top five and the fourth year you expect to win. Then, you have four years of experience to take with you, when you go on to the next level to compete—nationals."

"Four…years? Whoa," I couldn't imagine putting Tom and my family through this experience for four years. The money, time, and energy Stacey had spent on pageants must be outrageous.

"Each year gets a little bit easier for your husband. Stacey must have read my mind. "Pageants are addicting." She winked. "If I was going to worry about any lady in this room–" She turned and we now stood shoulder to shoulder. "It would be that one." She nodded toward a woman in the corner, who sat by herself, minding her own business.

"That one? Why? I wouldn't have even noticed her, if you hadn't pointed her out to me. She looks like the girl next door, a real plain Jane." *Like me.*

Stacey was quiet for a moment. "That's what we call a sleeper. Each pageant has one."

"She doesn't have a lick of makeup on. Her hair is in a ponytail, and she's wearing a dull pant suit," I said.

"Yep, that's Mrs. Grants Pass. Her name is Holly Nelson. She never wears makeup, not even to rehearsals. But when pageant day arrives, beware. When you see her for the first time entering the interview room, you won't recognize her. She will be in full-face makeup. Her hair will be a perfect pageant up-do, and she will look glamorous. It's amazing. You'll wonder who the new girl is." Stacey laughed.

"You're kidding. Isn't that like cheating, or breaking some kind of pageant rule?" This day was getting stranger by the moment.

I really needed to talk to Mom.

"You won't see any judges here at the workshop." Stacey said in a warm and friendly tone.

"Yeah, but the director—" I said, thinking she held all of the power, and she would notice how we dressed and presented ourselves.

"The director doesn't have control over the judges. I suppose she could report back to them, but I don't think she ever does. It's really not relevant in the big picture."

Stacey, still staring at Holly, shook her head in amazement. "It sure takes gumption though, and a whole heck of a lot of confidence, but that's her strategy. She doesn't want any lady here to notice or be intimidated by her. She flies under the radar. You feel secure around her, because you think she doesn't have a chance to win." She leaned in. "And then you see her dressed up on pageant day and wow-whee! Look out. It shakes every contestant to the core for a few hours on pageant day."

"What about her?" I pointed in the direction of a black lady.

Stacey turned to look at her. "That's Lily Franklin. She's competed before."

"She has the prettiest complexion and the most beautiful hair I've ever seen." I tried not to stare.

Before I could ask Stacey more questions, the pageant director, Mrs. Geltner, swept into the room, a bejeweled tiara perched on her beehive hairdo.

I joined the other women as they stood and applauded, leaned over and whispered to Stacey, "Tell me she's not wearing a crown."

"It definitely sparkles." Stacey whispered back in a 'believe it or not' tone. "She's very eccentric."

We both giggled.

Mrs. Geltner wore an expensive white suit, one size too tight and high heels. A brooch pinned to her lapel glittered with fake diamonds. On it was a gaudy crown, positioned above the year 1990. Her blue eye shadow, thick black eyeliner, red lipstick and the way she carried herself told the whole story. She was living in her past glory days.

"Please, ladies, take your seats." She snapped her fingers twice in quick, crisp succession. Her staff scrambled to stand behind her, in case she might need assistance.

I snagged a seat on the aisle, saving the one next to me for Stacey. The air buzzed with anticipation.

"Welcome, welcome, ladies," Mrs. Geltner spoke into the microphone. Her gaze swept the room. A Botox smile grew across her face. "We have a lot to learn today,"

She clung to the podium, as if she didn't want to share it with the scheduled guest speakers. She obviously enjoyed the limelight, even if only for fifteen minutes. "Let's begin."

The first of several guest speakers in our morning session, strode to the podium, a tall, lanky man with dark, beady eyes and a thin, greased mustache. He was either pigeon-toed or had weak ankles, as he short-stepped it to the front. His light blue suit pants fell right above his ankles and his stark white socks peeked out.

"Ladies, ladies, thank you, thank you, calm down now," He held one hand out, palm facing us. "Calm down."

Had I missed the thunderous applause?

"Really, ladies. Please. All eyes on me." He stroked his mustache. He already had our full attention.

I turned my head to eye Stacey and she looked at me. I bit my lip at the expression of horror on her face. Whipping my head forward, I focused on the man to avoid snickering.

"My name is Cecil." He looked straight at Mindy Storm in the front row and pursed his lips.

"He thinks we are all into him." Stacey whispered behind her notebook.

I covered my mouth to hide my gasp. I redoubled my efforts to listen to Cecil.

The man had a hangover *and* a comb over. He kept us entertained with his histrionics, explaining each contestant had her own section in the official program. Like a used car salesman, he explained how to sell our individual ad-pages featured in the book.

159

"Your section could be as small as the mandatory one page or as many pages as you can sell to sponsors. This will help offset your pageant expenses." Cecil took a moment to peruse the room, before he proceeded to give tips. "Remember ladies approaching business owners is good pageant practice."

Stacey wrote a note on a piece of scratch paper and handed it to me. "*Or you can get a job and sponsor yourself. It's easier.*"

I scribbled back, as a smile teased its way onto my lips, "*Or marry a millionaire who supports your every whim.*"

Cecil left the podium, during the applause. A weak response—more like a sympathy applause.

Mrs. Geltner stepped up to the microphone. "Thank you Cecil. Now please welcome Aimee."

Aimee floated to the front of the room and I settled back in my seat, ready to enjoy hearing from someone who didn't remind me of a silent movie villain. She looked twenty-something. Her body was fit, as if she lived in the gym.

"I was twelve years old when I entered my first beauty pageant," she began. "My mother paid a pageant coach and the first thing she did was put me on a strict diet." Aimee looked up toward the ceiling and swallowed. "After the first coaching session, when we arrived home, my mother dove into the kitchen cabinets. She removed all of the junk food, stored it in one cupboard and padlocked it."

Her smile, between sentences, showed deep pain. "That made my siblings angry at me because now they couldn't eat cookies and chips whenever they wanted. They punched me in the arm or tripped me every time I walked past them in the house, chanting *Fatty, fatty, two by four, can't get through the kitchen door.*"

Aimee wiped her eyes. "I sat in my bedroom for hours to avoid them. Then one day, alone in my room, something in my mind snapped. I knew I had to win the pageant to prove to my siblings, that all of the suffering I had put the family through was worth it. That moment, that thought, was the beginning of my eating disorder."

She paused and allowed her words to sink in. "On that day I started to deprive myself of food and continued until pageant night. I won my pageant. But believe me a lifetime of battling food is not worth it." She hung her head and took a deep breath before looking back to us. "I should mention when I started that diet," she air quoted the words that diet, "I was only twelve years old and ninety-five pounds. By the time pageant night arrived, I weighed eighty-three pounds."

I sucked in my breath, hearing the same reaction from the women in the room.

Aimee's voice softened, "Please, ladies. Be careful during your pageant season." With her closing words, clapping erupted.

Mrs. Geltner walked to the podium, clapping. She touched Aimee's shoulder. "Thank you, Aimee, for sharing your story. Ladies, that ends the morning portion of our program. Lunch is served in the next room."

Stacey, my new best friend, hooked my arm and we entered the room together, taking seats side by side at one of the tables for ten. My mouth watered at the salad course and I dug in.

No one would mistake my appetite for an eating disorder.

Before long, I noticed everyone in the room sneaking looks at Mindy, who sat at the next table. A lady across from us whispered, "Did you see her tattoo?"

"That is so not pageant-like. Right on her calf, too," another one said.

A blonde huffed, "I tried to sit beside her, but right then, she put her purse down on the seat so no one could sit there."

"How old were you when you entered your first pageant?" I forked salad into my mouth and looked at Stacey. With her bleached blond hair, veneers, and heavy makeup, it was impossible to tell if Stacey was younger or older than me.

"I'm forty this year." She gave me her best lip-glossed smile. *Good older than me.* This could be to my advantage, but since I like Stacy I didn't want to seem competitive with her.

"Why, are you nervous?" Stacey wiped her mouth with a napkin.

"Not really," Stacey probably saw right through me. "Okay, a lot." My chest heaved and I gave Stacey a sheepish grin. I was comfortable enough with her to be real and honest.

"Just have fun and be yourself."

Be yourself? Why does everyone keep saying that? Be yourself. Not one lady here is being real.

"Are you serious? Are we in the same room? These women all look like perfect clones to me."

"Just know who you are and what you stand for. Don't try to be like anyone else. Be yourself," Stacey repeated.

"Show me one person here who is her *real* self," I said. "Everything about them is fake." *That was harsh. I was becoming the stereotypical pageant woman.* I scanned the room again, enchanted by the bright colors of pageant suits and perfectly groomed women. I tucked a stray strawberry strand of hair behind my ear.

Stacey was undaunted. "Aside from all of the makeup and hairspray, just don't change your belief system. That's all I mean."

I pushed vegetables around on my plate and laid my fork down, too nervous to eat. "I'm anxious about picking our rotation numbers today. I'm really worried I'm going to draw number one." I fidgeted in my seat. "If that happens, I'll be the first contestant on stage, the first contestant to speak, the first contestant for everything." I pushed up my glasses with my pinky finger.

Stacey flipped the air with her hand, "Don't worry about it. That won't happen. What are the chances of that anyway?" Stacey's voice went up in pitch. She showed no concern on her face. Her perfectly shaped eyebrows didn't even rise.

"One out of twenty-eight," I answered without hesitation.

"Exactly, one in twenty-eight. It's not going to happen. Calm down." Stacey speared a carrot and popped it into her mouth.

"I know, but it's this intuition I have. I'm sure I'll pick number one and be the first contestant for e-ver-y-thing."

"First of all, Lucy, it's not the first contestant for everything. During the private interviews, the first five ladies start at the same time." Stacey leaned closer. "I'll tell you what. If you do pick number one, I will help you get through it emotionally. Believe it or not, some contestants want number one. That way they set the standard. They can raise the bar high and everyone who follows has to be as great or better."

"Nobody wants number one," I insisted, sticking to a theory which seemed obvious to me.

Stacey didn't respond. Lunch ended and we made our way back to the conference room.

Mrs. Geltner cleared her throat at the front. "I have an important announcement to make." We turned toward her in anticipation.

"For the first time each contestant will wear identical aerobic outfits for the swimsuit portion of the pageant. That means no swim suit will be worn during competition." She paused. "The name will change from 'swimsuit' to 'fitness competition.' We will order a black, one-piece unitard for everyone. You may pay by cash or check today."

The room buzzed as soon as she moved away from the podium and her staff handed out order forms. Stacey puffed out her cheeks, "Looks like the chunky contestants got their way after all this year."

Around the room most of the ladies groaned and grumbled and complained. They already had swimsuits chosen and purchased. I had waited to purchase one because I needed to lose more weight first. Sweet, one advantage for me.

When we finished filling out the order forms, a lady in her mid-fifties joined Mrs. Geltner at the podium, her lipstick perfectly matched her elegant pink suit jacket. She announced her credentials as a color specialist and makeup artist, another confident woman in the room.

I raced to take notes on her free advice. Mom would be so proud. The specialist warned us not to choose wardrobe colors which would make us look pale or washed out on stage. Then she delved into makeup tips. It sounded more like a well-rehearsed sales pitch than advice, but I did learn a lot. For example I should wear false eyelashes only for the on-stage portion of the pageant, and not for the private interviews.

The last guest speaker for the day was the judges' coordinator. He dressed like a CPA. He instructed us on category scoring, point calculating and the auditor's role. The contestants will not know who the judges are until receiving the program book at the beginning of pageant weekend.

The workshop drew near to a close with only one more item on the agenda…

The dreaded drawing for contestant number order.

~SIXTEEN~
It's All in the Number

Mrs. Geltner, the pageant director, reached into the podiums built-in shelves and drew out two black, velvet bags. She held the bags high in the air like she possessed a winning lottery ticket. They looked deep, similar to those used at church every Sunday to collect the congregation's tithes and offerings.

I nudged Stacey with my elbow. "What's in the black bags?" My eyes followed Mrs. Geltner, not wanting to miss a clue.

"Ping-pong balls, each are numbered, one through twenty eight."

As if she heard our conversation, Mrs. Geltner, held up one ball for show and tell. "Ladies, it's time to draw the contestant number order."

"Stacey, why are there *two* bags?" Confusion trickled through my voice.

"The first bag of ping-pong balls dictates the order in which the ladies will draw for their competition number," she whispered.

My gaze followed Mrs. Geltner's every move, as if she were on the verge of a magic trick. Maybe the ping-pong ball would turn into a dove and fly away.

"No matter how many times I do this, my stomach still turns somersaults." Stacey patted her tummy.

Mrs. Geltner started on the other side of the room, holding the bag for each contestant to pull a ball out. I pressed my palms to my temples, trying to understand what was going on around me.

"In this first round, most ladies want to draw a low number. Don't ask me why. Seems all the same to me." Stacey was now wringing her hands.

"Must be why everyone is happy over in that corner." I craned my neck their way, trying to hear what numbers were being drawn.

"You're up next." The director thrust the black bag in my face. I reached in and pulled out number twenty-seven. I did not know if that was good or bad.

Mrs. Geltner snapped her fingers in the air with her right hand and the room fell silent. "Every contestant has a number, right?" She put the bags down and adjusted the crown on top of her head. The ladies agreed in a chorus of lilting voices and heads bobbing.

"Next is the official draw. This round will determine the order you appear on stage," the director stated. "Now, who has number one?"

"I do." A hand shot up from the middle of the room. She had one chance in twenty-eight of pulling the ball with number one written on it. Now, I understood why everyone hoped for a low number in the first round.

Mrs. Geltner took the second black bag and waltzed to the contestant who had the first crack at the official draw. She seemed to enjoy the limelight and the power she held in her hands. She raised the bag above her head. "No peeking."

No one talked, whispered or even breathed.

I stiffened, perspiration tickling the back of my neck.

Holly Nelson, Mrs. Grants Pass reached into the bag and plucked out a new ping-pong ball. We were like little girls gathered around a gumball machine fighting over the white ones.

"Eight!" Holly said, with elation in her voice and a huge smile. She collapsed into her seat, air whooshed from her lips

I fought back an eruption of jealously. I wanted that number. Then again I wanted any number but number one.

Mrs. Geltner turned to her assistant, who stood a few paces behind her with a clipboard and pen poised above it. "She chose eight. Did you write that down?"

The former beauty queen across the room wrote the number beside Holly Nelson's name on the official form attached to her clipboard.

"Who has number two?" Mrs. Geltner scanned the room as another hand shot up.

Time slowed down. Fear crept over me, fear that I would draw the dreaded number one printed in black on the little white ball.

One by one, the balls were removed from that bag. "Who has number sixteen?" the director called out.

"I do." All heads snapped to Mindy Storm. I sat forward, as did several other ladies.

Please. Please pick number one.

Mindy grinned and tossed her head back. Her blonde hair flipped perfectly over her shoulder. If she was nervous, she didn't show it. I wanted to be like that. She pulled a ball from the bag and with a clear, even voice announced, "Number five."

In that second, the atmosphere changed. The whispers in the room sounded like the ladies all wanted the number five, simply because Mindy had drawn that number.

Whatever number Mindy pulled out of the bag, it would have been the one the others coveted. I could hardly listen as my chances of drawing number one increased with each contestants turn.

"Stacey, we're now at number twenty-one." My eyes watered. "No one has picked the first spot." I threaded my fingers tightly. I couldn't shake this terrible feeling in my heart. Maybe I was over-reacting, but if Stacey the calm, cool and collected one admitted to feeling queasy, then I was terrified.

"It's okay." Stacey patted my leg. "Seven more numbers left."

My heart beat faster and my breathing became shallow and rapid.

Calm down. Take a deep breath. Don't worry. This isn't life or death. Or even having a baby.

"That's easy for you to say. You already drew your number. Fourteen, remember?" I chirped at Stacey. "Right in the middle of the pack. What a great number." I pushed my hand on my leg to stop it from bouncing up and down like a jackhammer.

I doodled a daisy. Each petal the exact size and shape of the one before, hoping to keep my mind focused on something other than the number one ball. *Will I be the loser, who picks ball number one?*

"Twenty-five women have already drawn their contestant numbers," I whispered and gave a dramatic sigh. We both knew the chances of me drawing number one now rose to one out of three.

The contestants who already picked their numbers relaxed and visited quietly. Their giggles grew louder. *They weren't being considerate of those who hadn't drawn our numbers yet.* I tossed my pen into my purse. Doodled daises morphed into giant number ones.

"It's okay. If you do draw number one," Stacey leaned in, "I'll help you through it. I promise."

Great. She thought I would draw the dreaded first spot. I'm doomed.

I wanted to relax, engage in private conversations and enjoy this experience like the other ladies. I'd been robbed of that moment because I picked number twenty-seven the first go-round.

"Twenty-seven? It's your turn to draw, dear." Mrs. Geltner spun around to face me. I thought I saw red horns pop out from her head and fangs in her sneer. Only two balls were left in the velvet bag, the infamous number one remained.

I lifted my clammy hand in slow motion and reached inside the deep black hole. Like ping-pong balls, fear bounced up my spine. My fingers slid back and forth from ball to ball, taking time to feel each one.

The last contestant, who did not have her number, was now up out of her chair. I didn't want to take my hand out of the bag. If I took my time, I might magically know which ball to pull.

Dear number gods, be on my side.

The room became a pressure cooker. I knew everyone wanted me to hurry so they would know the results. I glanced at the lady who was waiting for me to determine her fate. She appeared helpless as she waited for me to pull the ball out of the bag. My eyesight became blurry. I blinked three times in an attempt to see her clearly. She was biting a nail.

Mrs. Geltner cleared her throat.

I looked at Stacey one more time trying to absorb any support from her aura that I could.

I shut my eyes and lifted my hand from the bag.

The past nine months had come down to this, a small round ball enclosed in my palm. If I had to appear on stage first, I would be forgotten by the time the last lady left the stage. I silently pleaded...*don't let it be.*

I let out a deep breath and unclenched my hand. Number one in big black ink. Crap! I opened my mouth to announce it, but the word stuck in my throat. Staring at the white plastic ball, finally I said, "One."

~SEVENTEEN~
One

The last contestant to draw after me, let out a deep breath and squealed.

I snapped my head down and stared at my daisy doodle. If I made eye contact with Stacey, I would cry. I didn't want the other contestants to see how miserable I felt. My nose stung and my eyes watered.

Don't cry. Don't cry. You can cry later.

My nightmare continued when the last lady cheerfully drew the only ball left in the bag, announced her number and avoided looking at me.

Mrs. Geltner turned on her heel and motioned to her staff to follow her to the front. "Ladies you have your contestant order now. From here on everything will be done in the order you drew." Mrs. Geltner and her staff said their goodbyes and we were dismissed.

The ladies were in no hurry to leave. They stayed chatting, the room sounded like a hen house. I bolted for the restroom, managing to slip through the door before a flood of tears poured from my eyes. I sobbed alone in the corner.

I don't have a chance to win. I've lost. I lost the pageant and haven't even competed yet.

The bathroom door squeaked open. I pressed my forehead against the cold tiles to hide my red eyes and flushed face. I didn't want whoever it was to know I was devastated.

A woman put her hand on my shoulder. "Lucy, are you okay? I'm sorry." It was Stacey.

"I can't be first. I just can't." I turned toward her brushing hair from my eyes. "I'm going to lose. Why even compete now?" My chin quivered as I fought back more tears.

"Don't say that. I know a lot of women who would actually like number one."

"Oh, yeah? Then, where are they?" I threw up my hands. "I don't see them following me to the bathroom, asking me to trade numbers. Sure, there's a whole line of ladies just clawing to be first." I couldn't stop the tears from flowing. I was angry. "Name just one!" I challenged. "Name one contestant who won a pageant after going on stage first."

Stacey didn't pause. She knew the Oregon pageant system's contestants personally, and all the past queen's statistics—like Adam knew the statistics on the back of his baseball cards. "Many, like Mrs. Newport, Oregon in 2003. Mrs. Corvallis, Oregon in 1988. How about Mrs. Medford, Oregon? She won in 1995. They all drew the dreaded number one."

I let out a mean chuckle. "Sure and how many contestants entered those pageants? Two?" I threw up the peace sign.

"Come on, Lucy, you have four weeks to prepare yourself mentally to be contestant number one. You can do it. Think of it as a good thing. You'll be the contestant who sets the bar. Set that bar high. Set it so high that the twenty-seven ladies following you will never reach it. Being first, it'll be out of the way and you can just relax and enjoy the show." Stacey laid her arm around my shoulder. "Imagine having to wait until all twenty-six performed before you. Your anxiety would be over the moon. It's way better to be first. I promise."

Ladies poured into the bathroom. They glanced at us then left as fast as they could, as if I had a contagious disease. If they stood too close or hung around me too long, they would catch a terrible case of *bad luck*.

"You know what's going to happen, Stacey?" I took a deep breath. "The judges will automatically score me a point lower than they think I deserve. They would have to, even if they love me. That way, it allows wiggle room to score another contestant higher. They can't give the first one on the stage a ten or even a nine. You can understand that, right?" My bottom lip quivered. "I'll be the first to brave the stage alone. Alone." My eyes locked on hers.

Stacey gave me a sad smile and dropped her gaze. "I told you I would help you get through this, and I will."

I appreciated her attempts to comfort me.

"Maybe number one won't be so bad after all." I forced a smile, through my wet tears. Though I didn't mean a word I said, I wanted Stacey to think her efforts weren't in vain.

Stacey hugged me, reached into her purse, fumbled through her things on the bottom of her bag, and pulled out a business card. "Here, call me anytime."

I blinked in surprise. *Pageant women had business cards.*

"I love talking pageant. I never get enough," she said with a grin.

I studied the flashy, glossy card she handed me. It had her pictured in her state banner. Her name and phone number were embossed in gold script. I flipped it over and read her personal motto: *Wardrobe frays, tiaras rust but pageant friends last a lifetime.*

"Do you have a card?"

I shook my head. "I didn't know pageant contestants carried business cards." We both laughed. My laugh sounded more like a defeated chuckle.

"A card will make your job easier when you walk into businesses and ask them to sponsor you. You'll look professional and serious when you ask them to buy an ad for the pageant book." Stacey crossed her arms and leaned against the wall.

"Oh, I like it." I smiled and put her card in my beaded handbag. "Thank you, Stacey. I'll definitely call you.

Besides, now I have to ask you how to purchase business cards."

Stacey's laugh was warm and full of affection. She gave me one more hug and left me alone in the bathroom.

I placed both hands on the counter and leaned into the mirror. "You can do this, Lucy. You can," I told myself. I splashed cold water on my face, fixed my eye makeup, reapplied face powder and walked to my car.

~EIGHTEEN~
Samantha

The shrill jangle of the phone made me yank the bed sheets over my head.

"I'm worried about Lu." Tom's voice carried from the living room, muffled by the bedroom door.

I strained to hear his words. He must be talking to Mom. I hadn't called her in days.

"No, she hasn't gotten out of her pajamas for two and half days, ever since the pageant workshop." His voice went in and out of earshot. "I don't know what to do. I've tried everything."

Yep, he was talking to Mom. I lifted my head off the pillow and held my breath so I could hear his words more clearly.

"She has hardly eaten, ran on the treadmill and the laundry is piling up." I heard his footsteps pacing in the living room. "She's really freaked out about being the first contestant. She said something more, about a lady who would probably win the pageant. I didn't quite catch her name Mandy, Misty or maybe it was Mindy." His voice became clearer as his footsteps approached the outside of our bedroom. He turned the doorknob, inched the door open and peeked in.

I pretended to be asleep.

He closed the door slowly. "No, she's still sleeping." His voice trailed behind him, as he walked back to the living room. "Lucy is worried about being first on stage for all of the different portions of the pageant, especially, the on-stage question."

I closed my eyes, replaying the pageant workshop day when I pulled the ping-pong ball out of the black bag. *Maybe, if I had taken more time with my hand in the bag, there would have been a different outcome.* "Why, God?" I swallowed back a sob. "Why?" I punched the pillow.

"I feel sorry for her," Tom said as he continued to pace. "I know…I agree. She's worried about nothing."

They knew nothing. I rearranged the pillow under my head.

"I don't know what to do. Any suggestions?"

Mom undoubtedly volunteered her ideas on the other end of the phone.

"No, I know she wouldn't want to see The Gang right now." Tom sounded defeated.

He liked problems he could solve but this problem was out of his arena.

"She definitely won't want to go away for a couple of days right now, either." A long moment passed. "That's a good idea. I'll call her right away. That might be a great surprise for Lu. I may have under estimated how important winning this pageant is for her."

One of Mom's suggestions must have stuck, like spaghetti on the wall. I put the pillow over my head, I didn't want to hear Tom and Mom talk about me anymore.

Nothing changed in the twenty-four hours since Tom and Mom conspired to change my outlook. My mood remained the same as the day I drew the dreaded number one ball from the black bag.

The doorbell rang and interrupted my depressive thoughts. I glanced at my clock on the bed stand. Noon.

It couldn't be that late.

Whoever was outside rang the doorbell over and over.

I hurried out of bed, pulled on a green pair of sweats from the floor and slipped into a solid colored T-shirt. I finger-combed my oily hair, pulled it into a ponytail, reached for the nearest bottle of body mist, sprayed it into the air and spun around to let the dew settle on me and my clothes.

"Coming!" I quickly stepped my way through the living room, let out a deep breath and cracked the door open. I squinted, to avoid the harsh sunlight. Once my eyes adjusted I realized who stood in front of me. "Oh my gosh!

Samantha Higgins? Samantha Higgins, is that you?" I squealed and threw the door wide-open, letting in the sunshine and Samantha.

Samantha wore stylish black slacks, a crisp white T-shirt, a Coach bag tucked under her arm and matching high heels, that made her look much taller than her five-four frame.

"Come in, come in." I hugged her, then quickly leaned against the wall to keep from collapsing on the floor.

Seeing my best friend from elementary through high school at my front door brought back memories. We had a trademark handshake, which I wanted to do right there in my living room. Grab wrists, pump twice, slide our hand to each other's, shake three times, then release, snap our fingers two times and yell, 'Whoosh." The memory made me smile. We shared all our dreams and fantasies with each other.

"What are you doing here? How many years has it been? Thirteen, fourteen since high school?" I opened the door wide and took Samantha's jacket and bag from her, then turned to the coat closet. The tight space reminded me of our hall lockers at high school.

Our lockers were side by side in high school, all four years, just as Sam and I were. We were inseparable. The teachers referred to us as "conjoined twins." If I wasn't at her house after school, she was at mine. We giggled about boys and dreamed about our futures. We shared personal things and I knew she could keep a secret.

"Let's go into the kitchen." I closed the front door. Every move Sam made held my attention. I couldn't believe she was actually here.

Our friendship had unraveled like a piece of cotton thread in an heirloom doily. It began one Friday night, our junior year, when Sam's father called. We sat on my bedroom floor in front of the full-length mirror, taking turns with the curling iron, putting ringlets in our long hair, before the football game.

Something had changed in her the second she hung up the phone. A look of disbelief and pain showed on her face. "My parents are getting a divorce," she said flatly. And that was that. She didn't say another word about it for months.

Sam's home life, as she knew it, shattered like a fragile china cup, which had been passed down through generations that suddenly tumbled from the kitchen hutch.

Sam touched my shoulder, "Lucy, your home is lovely," bringing me back to the present.

"Thank you. Are you hungry? I think Tom has some leftover pizza. I haven't cooked, in the last few days."

Searching the refrigerator for the pizza, I let my mind drift again. After the divorce, Sam fought with her mom over small things. She didn't trust her mom's loyalty anymore and Sam became skeptical of all relationships. She became increasingly sad every day. If she wasn't sad, she was mad. She was a walking firecracker with a smoldering fuse, ready to explode at any moment.

Brick by brick, Sam built a wall around her heart. Eventually she pushed everyone away, even me. I tried to convince her that I understood what she was going through. "How could you? Your parents are still married." She said. I made excuses to stop spending time with her.

The pain of her parents' divorce ran deep. By the end of our junior year, she took solace in the party scene. A scene I was never comfortable in.

Her parents lost control, distracted by their own problems and new freedoms. They hadn't notice the changes in Sam's life. Our friendship was strained, we simply drifted apart.

We had different views on dating. If she went out with the same guy two weekends in a row, she considered it a serious relationship. When I met Tom for the first time, I knew he was the one for me.

After our first date, I was happy to have Tom replace Sam in my life. He became the one I did my homework with, ate lunch with, and talked with on the telephone at night. Often, on weekends, we rented movies and watched them together.

Sam interrupted my memories, "Wow, you look great. You haven't aged a day, since high school."

"You haven't either, except you cut your hair." I took a step closer and fingered the ends. "It's short and simple and sassy."

"It goes with my job. I'm a divorce attorney now."

"A lawyer?" I laughed a pleasant you-got-to-be-kidding laugh. "I remember when you were kicked off the volleyball team because your grades didn't meet the school requirements. How did you make it through years of college? You have come a long way, Sam."

I removed the tin foil from the pizza and placed it into the microwave. The aroma of pepperoni filled the kitchen. Watching the soda fizz as I poured two glasses of diet pop, took me back in time to the many weekends we had movie night at my parents' home, before Tom.

"Pizza, just like in high school," Sam commented.

"Tell me more, are you married? Do you have kids? Where do you live?" I set the glass of soda in front of her.

Sam's eyes sparkled and her cheeks glowed, as she told her story. "I am married. Bradley and I met in divorce court. I represented the wife and he represented the husband. It was a lengthy case and when it finally ended he approached me in the courtroom nanoseconds later. She grinned. "He asked me out to dinner." Her face softened, as she quoted him. "'Any woman who can beat *me* in court is deserving of the best meal in town.' Bradley had the reputation of being the best divorce lawyer in the state, but I won that case."

"How romantic." I put both hands over my heart.

A sweet silence fell before she said, "We're moving back here."

I jumped out of my chair and gave her a big hug. "That's wonderful. We can do everything together again, just like we used to."

Immediately I imagined lunch dates, late night telephone calls and movies at home with popcorn and pizza, just like in high school.

"So, Lu, fourteen years is a long time. What are you up to, now? How are Tom and the kids? You have three, right?"

"Tom's the same as in high school. And, the kids are growing fast. Big news around here is, I'm entering a beauty pageant for married women."

She frowned at me. "Why?"

~NINETEEN~
Hear Me Roar

It's a pageant for married women." I said to Samantha with caution, tingeing at the word pageant.

"That's silly and outdated." She slapped the table, like a lawyer on a television show.

I grasped the sides of my chair. "Silly? Outdated?" I furrowed my forehead and echoed her words.

"You're telling your daughter and other little girls it's okay to be judged on the basis of your appearance and body shape. Is that really the message you want to send?"

"Samantha, you are stereotyping all pageant women and pageants. It's more than looks. I'm working really hard on my communication skills, running everyday on the treadmill and eating healthier." I sat up straighter with a tight smile.

As a lawyer, she could shred me in an argument. I braced for opening statement. "For what? So you can parade around in a bathing suit and be judged by the ideal 36-24-36? Lucy, women have worked hard and fought long to be judged the same way a man would be. Now, you're asking men to judge you, as you prance around on stage. It has taken at least forty years to change the public's mind-set about women."

She rested her case and I dug deep to defend myself. "There's not a bathing suit portion any more. We're wearing aerobic wear to showcase and encourage fitness." My argument sounded silly, even to me. Now I understood why pageant headquarters modified the swimsuit competition and changed the name to Fitness Category.

"Same thing. What would our mothers' generation think?" She shook her head.

"I'm working hard to bring attention to my platform and practicing public speaking. That generation of women would be happy that pageants provide a forum to express opinions on important matters, such as equal rights, if we choose." I tried hard to match my verbal skills with Samantha, the professional, liberated, and independent lawyer.

And to think, only moments before, I was hiding under my comfy, cozy covers, wallowing. Now, I'm up on a soapbox defending my position in a trial court.

"You think they're going to take you seriously in a swimsuit? Oh excuse me, 'aerobic wear.'"

I looked around the room. I didn't know what else to say.

"Is that what you choose to talk about, your platform? Equal rights?"

"Well, no. My platform is about *Early Intervention for Children Who Are Developmentally Delayed in Speech and Language.*"

Samantha's face softened. She looked down then looked at me. "Lu, I'm sorry. I forget. Entering this pageant must be stretching you."

She must be remembering all the times she stood up for me, when kids teased me mercilessly in school, about my mispronouncing words and being pulled out of regular English for Title One class.

"Remember that upperclassman?" Samantha punched the air.

"How could I forget?" I smiled. "You smacked him in the arm and shouted to stop making fun of me, or else." I laughed.

Her face lit up with a mischievous grin. "How about when I stuck a tiny garden snake in Trevor's locker with a note?"

"What did it say? Something like, 'If you don't leave Lucy alone, I'll knock your teeth out, and you'll be the one hissing like this snake.'"

"It was fun watching him scream like a little girl all the way down the hall and out the door."

We both chuckled at the memory.

Sam's expression grew serious and sincere. "I probably made things more difficult for you."

"No, Sam, just the opposite. All of the guys liked you. Since they liked you, and you liked me, they left me alone. It helped so much." Tears pooled in of my eyes. I looked out the window, then back at her. "It took years to realize what you did for me. Did I ever thank you for those times? You saved me from a lot of humiliation in high school."

"Stop." She swatted the air.

I placed my hand on top of hers. "You made it bearable to go to school. I'll never forget."

"You would've been just fine." Samantha's tone was serious. "Let me save you from humiliation again. Please don't enter this pageant."

"I'm in too deep." My voice was soft. "Plus, I want to compete. I really need to do this for me." I pulled my hand away.

It was Sam's turn to look out the window. "No matter how you package it and try to sell it, the pageant is about one thing and one thing only—outside appearance. The only diversity you will ever find in a pageant is blonde, blonder, or blondest."

She grinned and we burst out laughing. If she had been at the pageant workshop, she would have seen how true her statement was.

"Oh, Sam, it's so good to see you again." I planted one elbow on the table and rested my chin on my hand. "I've missed you."

"I know. I've missed you, too."

"When did you become such a feminist?" I stood to fill her glass with water. "I would never have imagined you as one. We were both cheerleaders. Remember those short skirts, snug tops and flirting with boys?"

"I remember but college changed me. It made me realize there's a much bigger world out there."

"Isn't feminism about giving women the right to make choices?"

Samantha sighed. We were both done talking about the subject.

My thoughts drifted back to a neutral subject. "Remember the miniature teddy bear with the half-heart charm necklace around its neck that read 'best', from ninth grade? I treasure it."

"I still have the other half that says 'friend.'" She gave me a hug.

Memories blanketed down to my little toe. "Let's make a promise. That we won't ever let so many years go by without visiting, okay?" I held up my pinkie.

"I promise." Samantha hooked her pinkie in mine and we shook. "It'll be easier to keep in touch now, since we're moving back here."

With new resolve, I changed into my workout clothes and hit the treadmill.

Six *Rocky* movie songs later, Tom walked through the office door and saw me running. "Hi, honey. Good to see you up and around." Tom took a step back.

"You're home early. I would give you a hug, but I'm all sweaty." I slowed down the treadmill.

"I wanted to see how you're doing." Tom pat my butt. "How's your day been, beautiful?"

"I finally accepted the fact I am going to be contestant number one." I hopped off the treadmill. "Back in action, ready to fight." I air boxed, singing, *Gonna Fly Now.* "You'll never guess who surprised me today."

"Who?" His shrug made him look adorable.

"Guess." I nudged him, a playful tone in my voice.

He loosened his tie. "Just tell me."

"Samantha Higgins." I waited for him to gasp.

Tom didn't say anything nor did he gasp. His expression revealed he knew more than he let on.

"You already knew, didn't you?" I spun my towel and swatted him in the leg. "Should've guessed you had something to do with her out of nowhere appearance, Tom Rupp. How did you find her? And, why now?"

"It happened like this," Tom stuttered. "I first looked her up because I wanted to surprise you at your birthday party, but she couldn't attend. So, I decided we would surprise you another time."

"Yeah…And?"

"I called her yesterday. Because you lay in bed for a couple of days and refused to get up, I thought you could use a visitor."

"You told her I was depressed?" My voice rose. "That I wouldn't get out of bed?"

"Not exactly." He back peddled.

"She didn't tell me you called her. So she knew about the pageant, that explains why she was well versed on the topic."

Tom rubbed his forehead. "I told her not to say anything. I didn't want to tell you, in case she didn't show up."

"Oh, so it was a sympathy visit at your request. It wasn't even her idea to come and see me. Is that it?" All the spunk drained out of me and I wanted to crawl back into bed.

"No, Lucy, it's not like that." Tom put his arm around me. "Sam was already going to surprise you by stopping by unexpectedly…someday. I just made the someday today. I thought now was a better time than later. You know, with you being so sad and everything."

"That was between you and me." I clenched my teeth.

"I couldn't stand seeing you like that, Lu. It broke my heart. I was desperate to do something. Besides your mom thought it was a good idea, too."

"What? You told Mom, too!" I crumbled, holding back hot tears. "Who else did you tell that I didn't get out of my pajamas for a couple of days? That I was depressed? Julie? Colleen? The Gang? Claudia? That's private! Nobody needs to know I was upset. How humiliating." I swiped at a tear rolling down my cheek.

Tom gripped my shoulders and forced me to look at him. "Listen Lu, it's not humiliating. I thought it would help you, and it did. Wasn't it good to see Sam? Lucy, you were smiling again." He released me and dabbed at my tears with his thumb.

"True. I'm so embarrassed."

"Don't be. I understand and I don't blame you for the way you feel."

"You're the only one who understands. You have seen me—"

"—Lived it," Tom inserted.

I chuckled. "Lived with me, through all of my hard work at losing weight, buying clothes, practicing 'The Walk' and everything else."

"Exactly. That's why I was sure you would be glad to see Sam. It's been years since the two of you visited."

I had to admit, I was glad to see her again.

"And you were happy after she visited you today, right?"

"Yeah, I was happy." I bit my lower lip.

"Okay, then. Don't be mad." Tom leaned in to kiss me.

"I'm all sweaty. You don't want to kiss me right now." I turned my head.

He crooked his finger on my chin, and turned my head back toward him. "I don't care if you're sweaty." His chuckle was warm. "Yes, I do want to kiss you." He gave me a tender kiss. "Now tell me all about Samantha. I want to hear everything."

~TWENTY~
Color Me Sexy

This dress is amazing." I pivoted side to side, studying myself in the mirror from every angle. My smile broadened and I pulled my shoulders back, fully appreciating my weight loss.

"It is beautiful, Lucy," Courtney said, circling me, "but it's red, red, red. To wear a red evening gown you have to be confident, bold and sexy." Courtney inspected my reflection in the mirror. "And you don't do sexy."

I wanted to do sexy. I wanted to do confident. I wanted to do bold.

"Are you confident enough to wear red? You're contestant number one, remember?" Courtney raised one finger along with one eyebrow.

Mom slid her pencil over her ear and took a step closer to me. "I love it. She looks stunning."

"Don't remind me about being number one. It'll just mean more work for you, is all." I did another full spin in front of the mirror. "Did you see the pageant website?" I changed the subject, but stole a peek at Courtney over my shoulder in the mirror. "My head-shot is the first one that pops up on the screen, because the head-shots are in the same order as our contestant numbers."

"Of course, I saw the website. Your headshot is stunning. Dusty Joe did a great job." Her gaze traveled up and down my figure.

I ran my palms down the front of the gown. "I like the two slits on each side. Backless makes it sexy and I love all the sequins."

"Those sequins make the gown heavy," Courtney shook her head. "How are you going to glide on stage, with a gown that weighs as much as you do? You may not be able to walk smoothly. You'll appear cumbersome. Have you thought about that?"

I was not to be discouraged. "I'll practice every day, I promise. Every day." I clasped my hands together, like a seven year old promising Mom to feed the puppy and take it potty.

"Every day. Gown and shoes." Her head bobbed with the words "gown and shoes." "Ultimately it is your choice, but I prefer the other gown, the blue one you tried on earlier."

"I appreciate that, but I love this red one, and I'm going with it." I placed one hand on my hip and twirled.

Mom flashed me a thumbs up.

Courtney gave me a weak smile. "You don't think it's too much with your red hair?"

"I'll color my hair."

"You can't. We already have your headshot done."

"I love this dress." I stuck out my lower lip.

"Okay, I'll do my best to help you pull it off." Courtney sighed.

At the register, I tucked the evening gown receipt into my wallet.

The sales clerk walked around the counter and handed me the garment bag. "Congratulations, Mrs. Rupp. It's a wonderful choice."

My heart did a back flip as the clerk handed me the garment bag. My arm dropped from the weight. *Had I made the right decision?* I turned from the cashier counter and almost collided with Stacey.

"Oh. Hi. What are you— how long have you been standing there?" I stammered. Did she see me buy my red gown? I didn't want any other contestant to see it until pageant weekend.

"Not long. You just now bought your evening gown? It's kind of close to the pageant date." If it weren't for the twinkle in her eye, I might have wondered if she was being catty. "Nothing like waiting 'til the last minute."

"This is my second go-around with wardrobe. Long story." I rolled my eyes. Stacey must have known she shouldn't ask to see my gown, and she didn't, a tacit agreement among the pageant ladies. She respected the secrecy of wardrobe. I appreciated that about her, and I knew she was a true friend. "We also found another interview suit today." I rolled my eyes again and hoped Courtney didn't see me. So far, I had two of everything.

Mom piped up. "That took the first half of the day."

"I feel like this is the second pageant I've entered, at least in the wardrobe department." I laughed at myself and pretended to be light-hearted, but in truth I was anxious about everything. All I did was think, breathe and sleep this pageant. "Stacey, this is my mom, Lucinda, and my pageant coach, Courtney."

"I know Courtney," Stacey smiled and nodded to her. "Lucy, you hired the best." She patted my shoulder. "Nice to meet you, Lucinda." Stacey extended her hand. "Lucy says such nice things about you."

I relieved my tired wrist and shifted my purchase to the other hand. "What brings you to the mall today?"

"I have to buy another pair of shoes to go with my gown. I always have two sets with me at the pageant. You never know if a heel is going to break."

"Two pairs? I'm going to take my chances with one. I can't afford another pair." I already had different shoes for the opening number, interview suit, aerobic wear and evening gown. "Tom is going to flip out when he sees the credit card bill." A twinge of guilt nipped at my conscience. I didn't intend to speak badly of Tom. The comment just slipped out.

"You need a job." Stacey's tone was adamant.

I stared at her, stupefied. "A job?"

"My whole pay check is solely for my pageant habit."

"Habit? You talk about pageants like it's a drug."

"Pageants are my drug." She laughed. "And, I needed a job to support it."

"I don't know why I didn't think of that. A job sounds like a great idea." My mind cycled through possibilities.

Stacey looked away and stared at the corner of the store.

"What is it?"

"My drug is tempting me, that's all." Stacey pretended to sniff cocaine from her acrylic pinkie nail, then gestured toward a rack of gowns. "That strapless gown is pulling me in." She outstretched one hand toward the rack. "Stop me. Help." She took a couple of steps then turned back around, laughing. "I refuse to give in. I need rehab. Pageant rehab."

The four of us laughed and the store clerk joined in.

"Well, if you don't buy two pair of shoes, at least buy two pair of nylons," Stacey advised.

"Good idea." I set the garment bag next to my feet.

Stacey leaned in and cupped one hand to the side of her mouth.

Oh, this is going to be good.

"Mindy is in the mall, too," she whispered. "This must be the day everyone is getting their last-minute wardrobe accessories." Stacey tskked.

"Really, you saw her? What was she wearing?" An anxious chuckle slipped out.

Stacey stepped back and shrugged. "She looked cute and professional in her black wool slacks, baby blue turtleneck and black short heeled shoes."

"What store was she going into? I want Mom to see what she looks like."

"I think she was leaving. She had her arms full. I waved to her, but she acted like she didn't see me. Not even a head nod." A sardonic smile escaped Stacey's lips.

"Don't worry, the judges will see how much of a dead-pan personality she has." I wrinkled my nose.

Before I said goodbye to Stacey, we promised to call each other throughout the upcoming weeks.

Immediately after Stacey left, Courtney turned to me, "Lucy this journey has been a lot of fun. I've done everything I can do. Now, we just wait for pageant weekend. Until then practice, practice, practice."

"Thank you for everything, Courtney. I can't wait, until you see me up there on stage on pageant night. I'm going to make you proud." I gave her a lingering hug, not wanting to say goodbye.

Courtney left, but Mom and I still had more errands on our list. We entered the tux shop to turn in Tom's measurements. A toddler mannequin posed in the corner of the store caught my attention. I turned to my mom. "How cool would it be to rent tuxes for the boys?" I strayed away from the counter to the small mannequin, "They would look so cute in the audience." I said, rubbing the polyester jacket.

She shook her head.

I was getting carried away. "You're right. That would be ridiculous." I needed to put a barbed wire fence around my sporadic ideas.

The saleslady finished with the other customer before helping with Tom's fitting form. Afterward I purchased slacks, white button-down shirts, and ties for the boys on clearance.

"Adam and Jake will look just as handsome in those clothes as in tuxes. No one is going to notice the difference."

Mom was right. The boys would argue later about wearing the ties, but they would...for me.

For Suzy, I found an adorable red party dress that looked a lot like mine. I wanted us to match as much as possible. I'd have to hide it or she would want to wear it every night before the pageant.

We soon realized we were some of the last shoppers. The storekeepers pulled down their cast iron gates and turned the Open signs to Closed.

My shoulders drooped. "Boy, I'm tired."

"Me, too." Mom looked at her shoes. "My feet are killing me. Are you as hungry as I am?"

On the drive home, I tallied the hours I'd been gone from my family once again. Guilt was becoming a regular visitor, but it fled, chased by fear and anxiety. Tom might be upset, but I hoped he understood how important these shopping trips were.

I dragged myself into the house, arms full of packages and my feet ached. All three kids were huddled together on the couch. They didn't bother to greet me.

Something was up.

~TWENTY-ONE~
Tuxedo

The kids weren't yelling, bickering or poking at each other. Instead they sat on the sofa unusually close to each other, smiling and laughing. A soft, fluffy, black fur ball curled into Suzy's lap.

I stepped closer to the sofa. "A kitten? Where did that come from?"

Tom barreled into the room carrying a ball of yarn.

"Isn't he cute?" Suzy's fingers stroked the kitten's fur.

"Hold him, Mom." Jake cradled the kitten from Suzy's lap and held it out to me, like a ball of black, wool yarn.

"Jake I can't right now." I shook my head and shot Tom an urgent look. "May I talk to you for a minute? In the bedroom." I high-tailed it to our room, arms still full of packages.

Tom followed me into the bedroom, his brow furrowed and his mouth in a tight line. I shoved the bags onto the growing mound in the closet.

I shut the bedroom door behind him, crossed my arms and leaned against it. "Tom? A cat? We don't do animals, remember? We never have and we never will."

"Now listen, Lu—"

I ignored his interruption. "Who's going to take care of it? Feed it? Clean the litter box? Because I'm not." I released a slow breath.

"Hold on, Lu." Tom held up his hand, "Just listen for a minute."

"No, you're not hearing me. I'm not going to be the one to take it to the vet, feed it and keep its shots current. I am not. Plus, we have a week long cruise planned. Who's going to take care of it then?"

"Please don't be mad." Tom gripped my shoulders. "Listen, you want to know why a cat? Because, you're never here anymore. The kids and I miss you."

His words brought my heart into my throat. I caught my breath, wiggled out of his touch, turned and said over my shoulder, "Don't you dare put this on me."

"A kitten will be a great distraction for the kids while you're rushing around town, spending our money, and talking on the phone day and night."

"That's not true, this again? Really, Tom. I'm always here, and when I'm gone, I'm just gone for a little while." I pushed my glasses back up the arch of my nose.

I hope I sounded convincing.

"How much money is in those bags you dropped in the closet? Should I remind you that's money we don't have?"

"Don't change the subject. This is about the cat, not money."

"Lucy, even when you *are* here, you're not here. Your mind and heart are not with us, the family. And, definitely not with me." Anger flashed in Tom's eyes.

"That's not true—" I squelched down the pain that his words might be right.

I loved my family. I was doing this for them too.

"Yes, it is. Your heart is in that pageant, and not here."

"That's not true," I repeated softer.

Tom closed his eyes briefly. "You were not here to make the decision about the kitten. You're not here to make us dinner anymore. You're not here to do the laundry for the family. If I'm doing all of the housework and going to work, then I'm making the household decisions from now on, without you, and that's that."

"You left me out. A pet is a decision I needed to have been included in. You took that away from me. Now, the kids' first memory of choosing a kitten is without me, their mom. Thanks a lot, I didn't even get a phone call." I ripped a pair of running pants and a cotton T-shirt out of the closet.

"Check your phone, I called you three times." He stared at me for a full five seconds, before he continued to speak. "This is not my fault. I'm the one coming behind you and cleaning up the mess you're making, because you're not here."

"Maybe, I'm glad to be gone. Ever think of that?" I paced across the carpet, jaw set. By his expression I knew I crossed the line with that comment. "I'm going for a run to be by myself."

"Lu, c'mon, stop for a minute." Tom reached out to touch my arm. "You are taking yourself out of our lives. Just go out to the living room and hold the kitten. Be a part of the kids' experience. It's their first pet. That's what they will remember, not that you weren't there to help pick it out."

"I hate cats. They shed." I whined, like a three year old forced to eat broccoli.

"They haven't named him, yet. Why don't we go out there, together, as a family and think of a name?" Tom lifted his chin toward the door.

"I have to admit, he is pretty darn cute." I shot Tom a sheepish smile, before we returned to the living room.

"Mom, we can't agree on a name." Jake shrugged and blew out a big defeated breath.

"I like Snoopy." Suzy petted the kitty's neck in Jake's hand.

"That's cute." I stroked Suzy's hair.

"No, not Snoopy." Jake tickled the kitten under its chin.

"He is adorable," I chimed in.

"Let Mom choose the name." Tom stood behind me, his presence forcing me to get closer to the kitten.

"Yeah, let Mom decide," they all said in unison.

"Well, it is a boy, right?"

They all nodded.

"And this family is in a pageant season of our lives, right?"

They nodded again.

"Aaand, Dad helped you get the kitten, and Dad is helping me in the pageant, right?" I looked at Tom with *I'm sorry* eyes and he telegraphed acceptance back.

The kitten dislodged from Jake's lap, I swooped to pick him up, looking him over. "I love how he is all black, except for the white on his feet and under his neck. How about Tuxedo? Tux for short?"

"I get it. Dad has to wear a tux on pageant night." Jake said, figuring it out.

"Tux. I like it," Suzy beamed.

"And the name will remind us of the year we adopted him," Jake added.

For the remainder of the night, we took turns playing and holding and petting Tuxedo. Despite my initial misgivings, I had to admit Tux was a great addition to our family.

~TWENTY-TWO~
Blue

Tom's long legs crept into my floor space and the arm of the seat pushed against my rib.

I hate flying.

As if Tom invading what little space I had wasn't enough, the back of the seat in front of me dropped two inches, when the occupant reclined.

Blue surrounded me. Blue headrests, blue carpets, blue seats, blue skies, and blue jeans. If the tight space didn't make me claustrophobic, then the monotone color would.

"How you doing, Lu?" Ron patted the top of my head, as he passed me on the way to his assigned seat.

A step behind him, Selena raised her eyebrows. "The kids will be fine. Don't worry."

I swallowed a sad laugh, trying not to worry. Determined not to stress about home. Determined to have fun with The Gang. Determined to enjoy my birthday gift.

My breathing became rapid and my head felt light. Black spots pulsed behind my eyes, I leaned back and concentrated on breathing evenly, unable to relax. I gazed at the cotton ball clouds, which dotted the blue sky. A peaceful vision of the kids plopped down in front of the television taking turns petting Tux filled my mind. This would be the longest time I'd ever been away.

I fished out a pageant magazine and thumbed through the pages. "What do you think Jake is doing right now?"

Tom kept his eyes closed. "Probably hitting his brother. Shhh, I'm trying to rest."

A hushed, muffled sound, followed by high-pitched child-like giggles interrupted my reading and made me miss my kids all the more. Chatter. More chatter, mixed with the color blue, and the swaying of the aircraft lifting, my insides curdled. A cough resonated over the chatter. It sounded like a sick cough, followed by "shhh." Then, more chatter.

"I wonder who is sitting by that cough. Do you think it's Pete and Julie, or Colleen and Mark?"

"I really don't care. Relax."

This plane is full of airborne germs that I can't escape. That's the last thing I need before the pageant.

I reached above my head and turned on the personal air conditioning. A chill crept through my pores at the thought of air pushing germs straight at me. I closed the vent.

The Gang, Tom and I, caught a shuttle to the seaport, tipped the taxi driver, and made it through the long lines and checkpoints to enter the cruise ship. Excitement warmed my chilled skin, my heart rate tripled. Thoughts of home, my responsibilities, and the upcoming pageant vanished, for a moment.

Tom and I, hand-in-hand, took our first step onto the massive ship and turned to wait for The Gang.

Ron stopped and pointed at Pete's tropical shirt, "You're the picture perfect tourist."

Mark also pointed at Pete, and bent over in a belly laugh. "He's right. You have a camera around your neck, wearing a straw hat, sunglasses, a perfect dab of white suntan lotion on your nose—" Mark couldn't finish his list he laughed so hard. Soon, the whole Gang joined in.

David stifled a chuckle then pointed at Pete's feet. "You're even wearing athletic socks with your sandals."

"Love those Hawaiian shorts, too." Colleen said. "Boy, it's not obvious you're going on a cruise."

"You look like Chevy Chase in the National Lampoon's Vacation movie," Tom said.

"Okay, enough from the peanut gallery." Pete laughed at himself. "Let's ask someone to take a group photo."

After we found a willing older gentleman to snap our photo we entered a fantasyland. Gleaming marble floors, a huge sparkling chandelier, a grand staircase separated by a twenty-foot copper replica of an anchor welcomed us.

We followed the thick red carpet past a large metal seagull, which hung on the wall. Our cabin was quaint. Perfect for two. I pressed my palm on the mattress then plopped onto it and bounced. *Yep, it was soft.*

Tom watched me, his smile growing bigger. "I have one more birthday surprise, then I'm done. No more surprises, no more spending money on you, no more commission check from the house sale on Alder Street." He made a motion like he was cutting me off.

"Thank you." I clapped. "This is the gift that keeps on giving."

"You can't thank me yet. You don't know what the surprise is. Besides it's not that big of a deal. It was more of a coincidence, but I'm going to take credit for it."

"What is it?"

Tom rested both hands on my shoulders. "For entertainment, on the last night of the cruise, they are holding a national pageant for teens. I thought you might like to attend."

"Oh yes." I gave him a rib-crushing hug. "You think of everything. Is the whole Gang going?"

"I don't think the guys are going. They're planning a Casino night, instead."

"I don't blame them." I smiled. "You can go with them, if you want."

"Nah, I think I want to check this pageant scene out, even if it is for teens."

Our luggage arrived and I hummed, while unpacking. One by one, my cruise possessions found a home: Tommy Bahama perfume, anchor necklace with matching earrings, and boat shoes. Drawers, shelves, and cupboards filled fast. I stuffed, stacked, and crammed belongings into every vacant space.

Tom laid down and flipped on the flat screen television. "I can't believe there is a flat screen on a cruise."

The bathroom mirror was nice with bright lights. In the mornings, before Tom woke, I could practice my pageant makeup.

"Let's go check out the ship and the running track. They say you gain an average of a pound each day on a cruise, with food available twenty-four hours a day," I said.

On the eleventh floor, we found the painted track lines. A posted sign read, "The track route is just shy of regulation distance." Only two running lanes, with lawn chairs lined up on both sides.

The sun-lovers reclined in their lawn chairs that snuck over into the lanes. People were everywhere, lined up like matchsticks in a box. I would have to make it work. I swallowed my disappointment. It wasn't Tom's fault the track was barely usable.

"On your right," a voice came from behind me, followed by deep panting.

Tom and I sidestepped to the left.

The shirtless jogger maneuvered through the sunbathers, kids, beach bags, and crewmembers, carrying trays of fruity drinks. Head down, shoulders forward, nothing was going to get in this man's way. I admired his tenacity to work-out on day one.

The next day, I awoke early, walked the flights of stairs to the track and went out through the double doors. I pulled down my warm-up sweats and revealed to the ocean my cute pink shorts and matching sports top.

I gazed out at the blue water and did a complete spin. Water, water, water. I spun again. No land in sight.

As I ran, harsh salty winds blew through my hair and chapped my lips. After an exhausting run, weaving in and out of lawn chairs, tourists and crewmembers, I promised myself tomorrow's run would be on a treadmill in the fitness room.

~

When we stepped off the ship at the port of Costa Maya, pillows of dark clouds hovered above us. By the time we arrived at the beach, the sun was in full shine and the wind carried the wonderful aroma of the ocean.

I laid my new beach towel on the warm sand to enjoy a natural suntan before the pageant. Back home the other contestants would have to bake in tanning beds.

"Tom, look at those ladies playing volleyball." My heart flopped to my toes as self-doubt crept in. "They should be entering a beauty pageant, not me. Who do I think I am?"

"Stop. We've talked about this a zillion times. We're on vacation. Quit comparing yourself."

"But, I'm still not at my goal weight." I pinched my side.

"If this pageant is going to make you think badly about yourself every time we do something, then I don't want you to compete. Period, end of story."

"Don't say that." I gritted my teeth.

"I just did. I thought this pageant was supposed to make you feel good about yourself. If it makes you feel more insecure, then I don't want you to compete."

"Fine. I love myself. I'm perfect just the way I am. Better?" I gave Tom a mocking smile.

"Actually, yes." Tom turned and brushed my bangs from my forehead. "Let's enjoy ourselves."

Within seconds, young Hispanic men and little kids, with big grins and friendly eyes approached us, trying to sell personalized bracelets, back massages and henna tattoos.

"Chicklets, Chicklets, Chicklets," a little boy sang, followed by a small girl, who looked as if she was his sister. They held little packets of white peppermint pieces of gum for a dime. I couldn't resist their innocent smiles with their missing front teeth.

"Tom, do you have change?" I held out my hand.

He reached into his pocket and pulled out a palm full.

I robbed him of all his dimes and bought one piece of gum. I turned to Tom, "They remind me of Jake and Suzy." I popped in the piece of gum. "Let's get back to the ship. We have a formal dinner to attend tonight. I must dress like a princess to enjoy my Prince Charming."

~

The last night on board, Tom and I sat near the front of the platform for the teen pageant and studied each contestant. I critiqued each gown, runway turn and on-stage question. I had my favorite girls picked out. Some had a mysterious stage presence about them and some did not. How did they get that? They were just teenagers.

The stage curtains closed.

"That settles that." Tom gave me a sly grin. "Pageants are definitely a sport for women."

I chuckled, stood on my tiptoes and kissed his cheek. "Thanks for sitting through this with me."

He returned a tender kiss. "Three hours, you're welcome."

Leaving the showroom, the bright lights, sounds of clinking coins, and energetic laughter drew us in to watch. "Tom." I tugged on his elbow. "Look at that roulette table. Have you ever seen anything like it before?"

Six players packed around the roulette table, each with their own designated color of chips. Orange chips were placed on most of the 36 red and black felt squares, with no less than eight chips per stack. "Which player has the orange chips?" Tom whispered.

"That one." I discretely pointed to an attractive older gentleman. "He just tapped the stack, so I think those must be his chips." A sixty-something man, who wore Wrangler jeans, black cowboy boots, and a white button-down shirt with a white blazer, appeared to be the owner of the orange chips. A woman, half his age, stood close to him. "I'm going to root for him." I held my breath, while the dealer tucked the steel ball under the lip of the wheel and sent it spinning.

The ball traveled around and around. I peered through the crowd on my tiptoes waiting for it to drop into a number.

Clink. It landed on red nineteen.

I scanned the table. Orange chips surrounded the number like ocean water enveloped the ship, but not one chip was on nineteen.

No one said a word for about three seconds. Then everyone moaned and stared at the cowboy.

He didn't react or flinch.

As the dealer scooped all the colored chips and cleared the board, the cowboy reached inside his blazer and pulled out five one hundred dollar bills.

The dealer exchanged them for more orange chips.

"Those chips are not dollars. They're five-dollar chips," Tom whispered in my ear.

The man laid the chips on the board with no apparent logic. The lady on his arm stood without expression, as if it were a normal everyday occurrence.

The crowd of onlookers grew. People stretched over our shoulders, as the excitement built.

The dealer sent the ball hurling again. It slowed to a crawl, bounced around the numbers, and rattled into a home box. "Seventeen."

Again, a number with no orange chips.

A lady player squealed with delight, as her one chip on the lucky number paid off.

The cowboy didn't look at her. He remained expressionless. He reached into his pocket and pulled out five more one-hundred-dollar bills.

This ritual happened over and over. His only reaction was to wink at his companion.

I canvassed the room for hints of a film crew, positive I'd been sucked out of real life and plopped into a movie. Five hundred dollars per spin. He was either crazy or mega rich or both.

"Early flight in the morning," I said to Tom. Reluctantly he and I moved slowly away from the excitement and walked back to our room.

"That was a lot of Ben Franklin's vanishing in one night."

"It was exciting to watch."

"All I could think about was the long hours of hard work the cowboy had to put in to earn those bills, and then poof, curtains closed and the money gone." Tom snapped his fingers.

"What are you getting at?"

"Like the pageant. All the hard work and money spent, for what? The audience gets a thrill. The system makes money. The winner wears a crown but if you lose, like the cowboy, what do you gain? Embarrassment?"

"I'm not going to be embarrassed, unless I trip on stage. I've learned a lot."

"Like what, Lu? How to apply stage makeup? Walk in high-heels? It all seems ridiculous to me."

"I thought you were supporting me." I looked at the waxed, marble floor leading to our room.

"I am. Sorry, just sometimes I wonder. That's all."

"Me too, I understand. Pageants are probably something most men won't ever understand." I frowned. "Just chalk it up to being a girl thing. A sport for women, remember?"

Tom pulled out the room key. "This is it, the end of our vacation and your birthday." Tom nudged me.

"It was all so perfect…except for you getting seasick." I nudged him back.

"How about the five pounds you gained?"

"That's not my fault." I stopped, stood and stomped my foot with hands on hips. "You're the one, who went to every buffet and order three desserts at every dinner."

Tom wrapped his arms around me and pulled me in. "I told you, Lucy, I don't care about your weight." He kissed my forehead. "Tomorrow, we will be home and you can start pageant prepping again."

I was anxious to see the kids.

I was anxious to run on my treadmill.

I was anxious to start my new job, which Tom didn't know about…yet.

~TWENTY-THREE~
Job

The UPS truck rolled down our driveway. I swung the front door open and waved as the driver leaped down from his seat. I watched him load boxes on to his hand truck. My supplies had finally arrived.

"Those look heavy," I halfway apologized to the young man in his brown uniform.

I held the front door open while he maneuvered up the steps. The realization hit me. I now had a job. I swallowed and tried to slow down my over-active mind. I couldn't wait to tell Stacey I took her advice and found a job that would bring in extra money to help pay for the pageant.

"Where would you like them?" He looked around the crowded living room.

"Over there." I gestured toward the couch. He unloaded three boxes in front of the television.

"That's perfect." I signed the computerized gadget with the plastic pencil. Once the door closed behind him, I dug into the boxes.

I scattered plastic packing peanuts. I spread the contents around on the floor, and breathed in the heady smell of new paper. Once the boxes had been emptied scrapbook supplies covered nearly every inch of carpet. Now, to work on creating a demo album I would use to show how to preserve family photos in acid-free albums, assuring my clients their pictures would last for generations.

Thoughts of clever ways to make money raced through my mind. Ideas began deep inside, teaching classes and selling scrapbook supplies in homes to friends and family. It was a sure bet, unlike the gambling cowboy on the cruise ship.

My favorite Cher CD played as I poured a diet soda and sat down on the floor with a shoebox full of family photos. I organized them in chronological order, just like I'd been taught. Hopefully, Tom will be proud of me when I place my first order with the scrapbook company and receive my first monthly check.

With pinking shears in hand, I trimmed the first photo into an octagon shape and studied it. The same photo that started this pageant journey. The photo I found months ago of me and Tom, arm-in-arm, strolling down the coastline. This time, I wasn't devastated, with twenty pounds shed and an updated wardrobe.

I jumped up, photo in hand, darted to the bathroom and taped it to the inside of the medicine cabinet. My *Daisy*

Dukes, an inspiration of where I planned to be again. *Almost there, Lucy.*

Planting myself back on the floor, I cut and pasted pictures for my dynamic demo album. I included a few photos of Tuxedo, so ladies without children could be reminded they needed albums, too.

I had barely closed the album, when Tom and the kids walked through the door.

"What are you doing?" Toms gaze swept the floor covered with scrap paper, acid-free pens and adhesive tabs.

"Wow, Mom." Jake skidded to a halt. "What are all these colored pens?" All three kids lingered around the colorful supplies.

"Don't touch anything, okay. After you take care of your backpacks you can have a popsicle, outside." I listened to the sounds of three pairs of feet pounding to their bedrooms.

Alone with Tom I smiled. "I wanted to surprise you with a finished product. Sit down and I'll explain."

Tom circled the living room and sat on the edge of the couch. He loosened his tie and studied the chaos at his feet.

Tuxedo popped out from under a throw pillow and climbed on Tom's lap.

"These are special albums." I held one up like a Barker's Beauty. "With acid-free pages and accessories to help prolong the life of treasured photos."

Tom scratched behind his ear.

"So these albums will keep your memories alive for years to come."

After I finished my sales pitch, Tom just sat there. "I get it. You want to preserve your pageant photos. That's okay."

"Yes and no." I swallowed hard. Time to reveal the entire scheme. "You are looking at a new scrapbook demonstrator." I held up my nametag with the company logo imprint. "I'll be selling supplies and teaching classes about creating memorable albums."

"Teach classes?" He furrowed his eyebrows. "Where are you going to do that? And, why?"

My heart jumped a beat. This wasn't going quite as I had planned. "I'll start at a friend's house. Maybe Selena or Colleen will host a scrapbook class. They'll need supplies and have to place an order with me. I'll earn extra money to help offset the expenses of my pageant."

One glance at Tom's face told me he wasn't on the same page with me. He fingered the album that now sat open on his lap. "You're going to do what?"

"I'm a demonstrator. I'm going to sell album supplies." My enthusiasm fizzled out like an open can of day-old soda.

"Can't people buy supplies at a craft store?" He asked.

"They can," I agreed. "But they need someone to teach them how to make the albums. There are a ton of ladies who have no clue how to preserve their family treasures. I can help them with that. Plus scrapbooking is a growing trend."

"Exactly when do you think you will have time for that?" His eyes, when they met mine, trickled with anger. "You aren't home now, as it is. There you go again, always jumping into things, without talking to me first."

"I want to help pay for my pageant and buy extra things I need, guilt-free."

"No, you don't. You just want another reason to be away from home and your duties."

"That's not true, Tom. That's not my motive. I don't want to feel bad about spending your hard-earned money."

"You think money is the only issue?" He let out a soft huff. "Where did this crazy idea come from?"

"From Stacey," I matched him gaze for gaze. "She works to pay for her pageant hobby."

"You're full of surprises today, aren't you?" Tom brushed Tux to the floor and walked toward the kitchen. He stopped and spun back around. "How much did that scrapbook kit set *me* back?" He rubbed his two fingers and thumb together. "You had to have signed up to be a demonstrator before we left on the cruise, and you didn't tell me. Five full days together and you didn't think to tell me? This is crazy."

My body deflated like a helium balloon and in a blur, I picked up the supplies and dropped them back in the boxes. "I'll start tomorrow. You'll see. I'll schedule some home classes and sell these supplies." I put a packet of colored paper on top.

"You didn't answer my question, Lu." Tom shouted from the kitchen, as he opened the microwave and thunked a frozen dinner on the carousel. "How much did all this cost?"

I let out a gust of breath and did not answer.

Tom ate his dinner on a TV tray watching the news, while the kids and I ate hot dogs at the kitchen counter.

While loading the dishwasher the front door opened and Claudia stepped in without knocking, "I have home-made double chocolate brownies."

"Aunt Claudia's here! Aunt Claudia's here!" Suzy jumped down from the bar-stool, skipped over to hug her knees.

"Brownies. Thank you, Aunt Claudia," Adam darted for the treats, Jake close behind.

"You didn't have to do that." I took the plate and turned toward the kitchen. "I'll serve everyone a piece, you'll join us?" I gave Tom a how-am-I-suppose-to-resist-these, look.

Claudia pointed to the empty, plastic, dinner container left on the TV tray. "That's what you had for dinner tonight?"

A pang of guilt raced through my heart. I braced myself at the kitchen counter, waiting for Tom's response.

"Sort of, I had a late evening at work and I wasn't hungry anyway."

"What did you have for dinner?" Claudia asked me, her eyebrows raised.

"Same. I was busy today." I handed Tom a brownie.

"Doing what?"

"I started a new job." Might as well try to setup my first class with Claudia. "I was hoping you would let me come to your home and teach your church friends how to scrapbook."

"If you went to my church, they would be your friends too." She looked at Tom, who conveniently had his mouth full of a brownie.

For once I wished Claudia wouldn't try to convert us to her church. "Please, Claudia, can I just come over and teach a class to your friends?"

"Oh a home-based company, you do all the work and they make all the money. Housewives work for free. You'll earn just enough money to pay for your gas and supplies."

Her words kicked the air out of my lungs.

I hadn't thought of that. Maybe I did blow it again.

I took brownies to the kids on the couch. A chorus of "thank you's" broke out.

"You're welcome." Claudia gave an I'm-the-best-Aunt-ever smile, picked up a brownie, and sat at the table. "Lucy, join me with a brownie?"

"No thanks, Claudia. You know I'm on a diet."

"Lucy, one brownie is not going to hurt." She picked up the chocolate square. "Look at me…size ten. I'm not fat and I eat them dusted with powdered sugar."

I took a bite-size brownie. "I guess one won't hurt."

They did look good, but just once I wished she'd support me.

Before Claudia finished her last bite, I dug to the bottom of my supply box, found invitation postcards for a demo class, and tried to hand them to Claudia.

When she saw them in my hand, she showed me the palm of her hand. "Stop, sorry Lucy. I want to keep my friends as friends. I don't want them to feel obligated to buy something they don't want."

"But, Claudia. They will want these albums. They preserve pictures for a lifetime. Please."

She sighed. "Tell you what, if you are still selling the supplies in six months, I'll let you teach a class. Okay?" She gave the kids each a kiss on the forehead before leaving.

After closing the front door behind her, I met Tom's gaze and nodded toward the bedroom.

He followed me. "What?" Tom sounded defensive, closing the bedroom door.

"Your sister, of all people, should understand how important it is to preserve family photos. Your parents are gone, and there are only a handful of photos of them. Doesn't she know she should take special care of the pictures? She just doesn't want to see me succeed."

"That's not true, Lu." Tom pulled me in for a hug.

"Yes, it is." I took a step back. "Why did she bring brownies? She wants me to break my diet. You heard her. And she threw in a dig about the frozen dinners, because she knows I'm no Martha Stewart."

"Claudia is just being protective of me. Remember, she took Mother's place after she died." A rush of tenderness filled me. He continued, "We've been over this a zillion times. You know Claudia likes you. She's worried the pageant is taking you away from our family. Don't fret over things she says. It does no good, and it doesn't change anything, you're still competing in the pageant."

"It's not that easy." A sob left my throat. "She makes me feel like I'll never be a good enough wife for you."

"Do you want me to talk to her?"

"No, that will make things worse. Claudia would think I put you up to it."

Tom rested his forehead on mine and whispered, "I know she's been hard on you. Thanks for trying to help pay for the pageant expenses. I hope it works."

"I can't believe she won't host a demonstration in her house."

"You should have launched a brownie bomb at her." Tom chuckled.

~

The sun hid behind the morning clouds, the air was crisp. I gathered my demo album and supplies, and loaded the back seat of the SUV. I would prove to Tom I could sell albums.

I drove to the only friendly lady I thought of who would have time to work on an album, possibly interested in preserving memories and had the money to buy scrapbook supplies. I hoped to sell an album and accessories today. My skin prickled thinking about it.

Dear old Mrs. Abernathy, the first person in the sanctuary every Sunday morning, sitting on the right side of the room, first pew, reading her Bible. She was widowed recently. Surely she had photos of her late husband she would want to keep in a memory book.

First sales pitch, my insides twisted as I walked down Mrs. Abernathy's brick sidewalk with the demo album under my arm. I took a deep breath, then knocked.

Mrs. Abernathy opened the door with a warm smile.

I stepped into her foyer and detected the smell of mothballs coming from her coat closet. I held back a sneeze. One look at her outdated living room told me I would have a hard time selling her anything. It didn't look like she had made a single purchase in the last two decades.

"Mrs. Abernathy, I apologize for not calling before I dropped in, but I'm excited about this new project and you were the first person I wanted to show. I teach classes about how to preserve memories."

Coo-coo, coo-coo. A little wooden bird popped out from her kitchen wall clock.

"What? I'm sorry, I didn't hear you over the bird. Did you say you are reaching to the few? You need some money?" Mrs. Abernathy pushed a stray strand of hair behind a bobby pin, which was holding her silver locks in a bun.

"No, Mrs. Abernathy." I looked down. "I said I have a new job, I'm teaching."

"Honey, you may show me what you're selling, but why are you working and not at home with your husband and children?" She tskked.

She must be stuck in an *Ozzie and Harriet* episode. I cleared my throat. "I'm working to earn money for a beauty pageant I've entered." I quickly clapped my hand over my mouth.

"A beauty pageant? Oh, dear. Pageants are so worldly. Why would you want to do that? Your poor, poor husband." She shook her head disapprovingly.

She must not know about the other lady who attended our church and won the state pageant a year ago.

This was going to be a hard sale. "Can I show you the albums and the supplies?" I asked in my sweetest voice.

"Have a seat, Lucy."

I sat in her stiff, wingback chair.

"First of all, explain to me why you would want to put yourself on stage for everyone to judge your appearance?" She took her place across from me. "You know God looks at the heart and not the outer beauty. Beauty is fleeting, dear one. The last thing society needs is more affirmation that a woman is only as valuable as she is beautiful."

"Not to be argumentative, Mrs. Abernathy." I refrained from rolling my eyes and thought fast of the beautiful, young, Jewish orphan in the Bible. "But Esther competed for the love of the king."

An awkward silence fell between us.

I plunged on. "Esther prepared for a year before she went to the king, six months with oil of myrrh and six months of perfumes and cosmetics." A soft huff commanded my muscles to relax. "While she was in the care of the king's eunuch, I imagine his people taught her how to stand, walk, bow, and even where to fix her gaze. I would love to know what lessons Esther learned that year. Wouldn't you, Mrs. Abernathy?"

Mrs. Abernathy's gaze fell to the coffee table where her Bible sat. "Signing up for a beauty contest is one thing. Being forced into one, like Esther, is another. I can image the commissioner checking Esther and all of the other girls' teeth, like a buyer would check a horse's. Can you envision it, Lucy?"

"The girls were probably swept up in the dreamy romantic glamour of it all. Just like me." I tilted my chin, put a hand to my chest and let out a gentle breath. "One of them was going to be chosen queen, and would wear the royal crown."

"Yes, Esther is a lovely story in the Bible." Mrs. Abernathy reached out and touched my arm. "It was her mysterious quality, which won the favor of Hegai. Much responsibility went with the title of queen." She shifted, her eyes brightened. "I never thought of it as a modern-day story. You will take this opportunity and teach your daughter about Esther, right?"

"Oh, yes. I promise, I will. Now, back to why I am here. May I show you how to preserve your precious pictures so they won't fade or yellow and last for generations."

Her cheeks went translucent, as if she was thinking about her late husband. "Yes, dear, you can show me. You just might be a God-send after all."

After an hour, she bought an album, supplies and set a date for a class in her home with her friends.

I stood to leave.

Mrs. Abernathy stopped me. "Lucy, one more thing." She moistened her thin lips. "How are you going to handle the rejection, if you lose?"

"I'm not going to lose, Mrs. Abernathy."

~TWENTY-FOUR~
Role Model

With only days left, I needed to fit in serious practice time. I gathered clutter from the living room, clearing a pathway, returning misplaced items to their new designated spots. I found several websites about organizing. I needed to, so my family wouldn't feel neglected, and Claudia couldn't complain.

Alone in my bedroom, I stood in front of the full length mirror and turned side to side, sucked in my tummy, and forced my heart back into its proper place from the bright, shocking color of the red evening gown I'd slipped on. Perhaps the longer I stood there, the more comfortable I would become.

Whispers of doubt swirled in my mind concerning my gown choice. There was nothing I could do about it now. This was the second dress I'd purchased and only a week to become acquainted with my bright, sexy, red gown before pageant weekend.

I slipped into my high heels, looked at the clock to see where the hands would fall in fifteen minutes, and glided out the bedroom door to my imaginary runway.

The click, click of heels on the hardwood floor captured my attention. Suzy appeared in front of me in her party dress I purchased for pageant night. Love washed over me when she stuck her hip out and tried to imitate my walk. I laughed. "Suzy, where did you get those fancy high-heels?"

"Grandma bought them for me," she answered with a big toothless smile.

"She did, huh?"

"Look, Mom, I'm practicing like you." Suzy boasted, while she hugged the kitten to her chest.

"You be careful. I don't want you to sprain your ankle. Why don't you let Tuxedo down?" I glanced at the clock. "I have eight minutes left of practice. You can follow me if you want." I stood straighter, still giggling at Suzy's imitation of me as we sashayed around the living room.

I knew I shouldn't, but I couldn't resist. "Suzy, do you want to play with my makeup? I'll put some lipstick on you." Tom might disapprove and Claudia, well, she would think I was pushing Suzy into becoming a diva.

"Can I?" She danced into my bathroom, ahead of me, before I changed my mind. Her eyes grew big as she studied the different colors of eye shadow, lipstick, and blush, neatly sorted and stacked in the trays.

"Sit still and I'll put a smidgen of eye shadow on you. What color do you want?"

Suzy carefully studied the colors. "That one." She pointed to the light-blue shadow. She closed her eyes, and I lightly swept the makeup brush back and forth across her eyelids.

Mrs. Abernathy's advice came to mind.

Now would be a good time to teach Suzy about Esther.

"Would you like to hear a story about a real queen?"

Suzy opened her eyes. "Yes, Mommy."

"Once upon a time, there was a girl named Esther." I swiped the brush through the blue shadow to grab more color.

"That's a pretty name."

"Yes, it is. Esther's mommy and daddy died, when she was young. Her cousin, named Mordecai, adopted her." I said.

"Just like daddy's mom and dad died and Aunt Claudia took care of daddy?"

"That's right. Well, one day, a king named Xerxes was looking for a new queen. Many young girls went to the king's palace to learn how to become a queen." I put down the eye shadow brush and picked up the mascara. "Open your eyes and look up."

Suzy did exactly what I asked.

"Now blink slowly."

"How long did it take them to learn how to be a queen?"

"About a year. Then, the women paraded in front of the king, and he chose Esther." I applied pink lipstick to her bottom lip. "Now, smack your lips together."

"Kind of like a beauty pageant?" Suzy opened and closed her mouth a few times, careful not to smudge her lipstick.

"Just like a pageant." I smiled at my work and handed Suzy a mirror. I needed a moral ending to the story. "Suzy, beauty is fleeting. That is why you need to be pretty in your heart, too."

"What does fleeting mean?"

"It means you get old real fast." I closed the different makeup items I had used, and watched Suzy admire herself in the mirror. "Time to take your party dress off and change into your play clothes."

"Do I have to take my makeup off?" Suzy beamed. "I want to show Daddy how pretty I am."

"Okay, that's fine." I gave a weak smile hoping Tom would tell her how pretty she looked.

Suzy went to her room to change into play clothes.

My stomach rolled at the empty suitcase lying on the bed. Mom would be proud of me, though. I wrote a list to remind myself what to pack. Now if I only knew where to begin. Deep in thought, I didn't hear Tom come home. He walked up behind me and tapped my shoulder. I jumped, "You startled me."

"You're concentrating on something," he said, with a hint of concern. "Is it being away from the kids for a few days?"

I turned and faced him.

He brushed a wisp of hair out of my eyes and tucked it behind my ear. I turned back around and stared at the empty suitcase.

"What's wrong? You look upset Lu. Talk to me."

"Mom said I should make a list of each outfit, the jewelry, shoes, and hair accessories, then check each item off as it goes into the suitcase."

"Lu, you're avoiding my question. This isn't about packing. Now, tell me. What's wrong?"

My chest constricted. "Last night, I had a bad dream. I've thought about it all day. Like I need another worry to add to my long list."

"It was only a dream."

"I walked out on stage still contestant number one. The Emcee held the fishbowl full of little, folded pieces of paper with questions written on them. I reached in, pulled out my question, and froze. Stood there, paralyzed."

"That's it? That's your nightmare?" Tom chuckled.

"Tom, it's a big deal. My dream went on and on. I stood on stage forever. My mouth moved, but no words came out. The audience sat there, staring, waiting for me to say something, anything. You should have seen the Emcee's face. He didn't know what to do. I couldn't wake up. It seemed so real."

"Lu, that's not going to happen to you," Tom stepped closer. "You're going to do fine."

"Tom, you know better than anyone that I don't use correct grammar when I speak. I've always relied on you to talk for me. You know how I struggle with pronunciation. I've learned to take shortcuts when I express myself just to survive in the world of communi—"

"Lucy, slow down. Come here." He wrapped his arms around me. "You want this too much. You have worked too hard to freeze on stage." Tom held me tighter.

"It's a big deal. What if I do freeze?" I pulled away, his efforts to encourage and cheer me up weren't working.

"You're not going to freeze. If you keep dwelling on it, you won't enjoy the experience." Tom blew out an exasperated breath.

I decided to let him think he was helping and making me feel better. "Okay, you're right. Thank you."

"That's better. That's why I'm here. You can always tell me anything." Tom stepped closer and kissed me lightly.

The phone rang. Caller ID revealed it was Stacey. I rushed to answer. "Hello, Stacey."

"Hey girlfriend," she said. "Are you ready for the weekend?" The excitement in her voice was contagious.

"As ready as I'll ever be. I'm trying to pack. Wow, what a chore this is." I looked back at the empty suitcase.

"I'm all done." The pride in her words were followed with brief laughter.

Of course you are. "Do tell. What's your strategy for packing?" I hoped she had a system I could copy.

"It's easy. I have several resealable baggies. In each one, I place the jewelry, hair accessories and everything I need for wardrobe changes. Then, I put a label on each baggie. One baggie will go with each of the outfits, aerobic wear, private interview, opening number, and so on. I take a hole punch, and put a small hole in each baggie just big enough to slip the hanger through."

Simple. There must be an organizing gene, and I didn't have one.

"I have a separate, oversized duffel bag I use for shoes only. On the bottom of each pair of shoes, I write on masking tape, the competition category. If you do that, remember to take off the tape in the dressing room before you go on stage. I also have a case, which carries everything I need for makeup and hair. It's simple, and it's really not that much stuff when you divide things into categories."

"Thank you, Stacey. It's so nice of you to share all your secrets with me."

"No problem. I learned from many trials, errors and blunders and a few expensive mistakes. I told myself, if I could ever help another woman avoid embarrassment, I would. Besides, I'm a believer in pageants and I want every woman to be a believer."

"Believer?"

"Most people who despise pageants will have no problem offering their opinion but being on stage saved my life. If I didn't have a pageant to look forward to, I would probably be locked up in some mental hospital, fat farm or I'd be house-bound."

I laughed at the thought of Stacey in a white straight jacket asking the warden if the color white made her complexion look pale.

"I love making new friends, having a goal, and basically, feeling younger. I've already decided I'm going to fight aging 'til the bitter end. I can't think of a better way than competing in pageants." Stacey voice came through light-hearted but clear.

Suzy walked past me, still wearing the makeup from earlier in the day. *Oh crap.* I had forgotten to prepare Tom about our makeup play date.

"Did you hear the news?' Stacey asked.

Oh, she did have a reason for calling me. "Hear what?"

I looked into the living room at Tom on his knees at face level with Suzy. He patted her head and turned to look at me.

I shrugged, giving him an I-don't-know-what-happened look.

Tom winked at me and walked over. "Like mother, like daughter, huh?"

Smiling, I nodded at him as I listened to Stacey.

"Mindy separated from her husband. She wants a divorce, but she's going to wait, because she wouldn't be eligible to compete in a married women's pageant."

"What? No way. Separated?"

"Yeah, and if she wins, like she thinks she will, she can't file for divorce during her reign, or she'll be dethroned."

Maybe Mindy would do the right thing and drop out. It would be one less contestant to worry about. "If they are separated, is her husband still going to escort her on pageant night?"

"I'm sure he will. It's my understanding he doesn't want the separation." She paused on the line. "But he also doesn't want to give up his girlfriend." Stacey laughed. "His guilt will cause him to show up on pageant night for Mindy."

Tom walked by me and whispered, "Our daughter is beautiful, just like her mommy."

I blew a kiss to Tom. "I can't imagine representing married women and being on the brink of divorce. That's odd to me."

"My understanding is, Mindy hasn't been home much while preparing for the pageant. That's her husband's excuse for finding a girlfriend."

I flinched. Lately, I had been gone too often from Tom and the kids. My stomach churned. I turned my back toward the wall and whispered into the mouthpiece, "How much time do you think she's away from home?"

"If she's like all of the other pageant women, a lot. The divorce rate is extremely high in pageants," Stacey said mater-of-fact. "This pageant system alone is running about an eighty percent divorce rate amongst the winners…and there are a lot of systems."

"Eighty percent?"

"They say the crown is the 'kiss of death.' The inside joke with ladies is, 'You win the crown, lose your husband.'"

"That's horrible. Is it really that bad?" I looked over

my shoulder to see if Tom was in earshot of my conversation.

"It takes a strong, confident man to stand next to his wife with the spotlight on her," she said with a little hint of sadness. "We can be divas at times, ya know?" Her laugh sounded forced. I think it was more for my benefit than hers.

"How can Mindy compete when she is separated? I mean is he really going to want to make the voice-over tape telling a full audience filled with her family, how much he loves her and what a great wife she is?"

Stacey sighed. "There's no proof they're separated or their marriage has problems. I only know this because it's a small town and the gossip flows like a relentless river."

"What about the pageant director? If she knew, she would send a letter to Mindy telling her she couldn't compete, right?"

"She won't do anything," Stacey said. "Mindy is just a number. Each number brings the pageant money. Believe it or not, directors usually spend more money organizing a pageant than making a profit. There is tremendous overhead. Mindy's participation will only help cover the expenses."

"Pageant weekend should be interesting."

~TWENTY-FIVE~
Registration

Make sure you do your homework," I told Adam and Jake. "And help Dad with the meals." I hesitated at the door and looked one more time around the clean living room.

Adam droned, "Yes, Mom. You already said that." Keeping his eyes glued to the basketball game on television.

"You kids keep your rooms picked up," I told all three of them, "and no fighting." I wagged my finger, and tried to find more things to say, in order to linger at the door. "Take good care of Tuxedo. Oh, and empty his litter box."

Tom touched my elbow. "Go ahead. Say goodbye again."

I dropped my bags and went to the kids for another round of hugs. "Be good." I looked away not wanting them to see me missing them already. "Bye, Suzy. Bye, Jake and Adam. I love you."

This was too soon to leave them alone. After all we just returned from our vacation.

"Don't worry, Lu," Tom assured me one more time, when he walked me to the car. "We have everything under control. Go and have fun. We'll be fine."

"I'll text and call you every spare moment." A soft moan rose in my throat. I pressed my key fob, opening the trunk, picked up my bags and headed down the steps.

Tom followed with two more bags. "Geez, Lu, it's only two nights and three days. What could you possibly have in these?" Tom flaunted a sideways grin.

"This bag is just shoes." I grunted as I lifted it.

"Please, don't remind me of how much money that bag alone is worth."

We both let out an awkward laugh and loaded the trunk.

"Come here." Tom wrapped his strong arm around my shoulders and pulled me into him. His other arm circled my waist. "I'll miss you," he whispered in my ear. He added a kiss. "Be nice to the other kids on the playground and behave yourself." Tom winked.

He looked down at me. "Remember, win or lose—"

"I know. I'm your queen." I gave him a shy smile and one last kiss, before I settled behind the wheel and drove off.

With my foot on the brake and both hands on the steering wheel, I stared long at the red light which blurred as tiny tears filled my eyes. I couldn't turn around, not now. I pushed my mixed emotions down into a cavity in my heart and concentrated on the task at hand. Operation Pageant.

I turned on the stereo and listened to the fourth CD in the *Verbal Advantage* set, "Secrets to Fearless Conversation," which Courtney had loaned to me.

Nobody could accuse me of not being prepared. Over the last nine months, I had achieved my goal of shedded dress sizes, mastered the art of walking in four-inch high heels, and rediscovered myself, the girl in the photo lost long ago. A wild cheer rose in my mind.

It was here. The weekend that took my energy, took my time, and took my money. The weekend that wreaked havoc on my relationship with Tom. The weekend which drove my family crazy. Pageant weekend and I…we were ready to collide.

Once at the hotel, I fought my way through a flood of beautiful women, who filled the grand lobby. They wore glamorous outfits, with sashes around their bodices, standing in groups of two or three, each waiting to register. The atmosphere was so charged I expected lightning to flash. Hotel employees wove in and out of the commotion.

My heart leaped, pushing away the memories of my pageant workshop insecurities, this time I was prepared. With an Ivana Trump aura and the knowledge of each contestant's social network bios I adjusted my sash and touched my perfect pageant hair. Not to be out-done, I had my share of hairspray, brown eye shadow applied in the perfect cat-eye shape, and a Jackie Kennedyesque wardrobe even down to the white pearl necklace.

"Lucy. Lucy." Stacey approached me from behind. "We get to share a room!"

Relieved, I gave her a warm hug. "Great. I still have to register. Will you wait for me?"

"Sure. I'll stand in line with you." Stacey said. She wore a Ralph Lauren Black Label, Sue Silk Georgette tank dress in red, finished with silver strappy high heels.

"You look wonderful."

"Thank you. And this…" Stacey spun in a full circle, "is why I work." She leaned in to me, "This outfit is just shy of a thousand dollars," she whispered.

I tried to hide my expression of shock. I shifted my weight from foot to foot to relieve the throbbing in my toes my new high heels triggered. Registration took a long time. My anticipation of receiving my pageant packet grew with each step closer.

I didn't recognize the lady in line three places ahead of me. She hadn't been at the workshop, and her profile wasn't one I had researched on the pageant website. She wore white capris with a navy blue, anchor crest, button-down collared shirt, accessorized with a white nylon rope belt and white dressy sandals. She looked as if she was next in line to take Kathie Lee Gifford's spokesmodel job in a Carnival Cruise commercial.

"Stacey, who's that?" My heart sank.

"Her? She just signed up to be a contestant. Her name is Carrie Campbell, Mrs. Ashland."

Those were exactly the words I was afraid I was going to hear.

Stacey acted like she didn't care, but when she pulled her shoulders back I knew the truth.

"Do you remember Mrs. Gresham?"

"Yes." My gaze fastened on Carrie, at the front of the line.

"She dropped out of the pageant at the last minute. If I had a choice, I'd rather compete against Mrs. Gresham."

"Did Carrie's headshot make it into the program book?"

"Yep. Headquarters will take the mockup program book to the printers today. They always wait 'til the last minute, for reasons like this." Stacey flipped her hand in the air. "Ladies join and drop out of the pageant at the last minute every year."

"But she didn't attend the workshop." I stated the obvious.

"Doesn't matter. Workshop is not mandatory, silly."

"It's not?" I'd never stop being surprised by the pageant world. "What do you know about her?" I shifted on my feet again, and wiped my sweaty palms on my thighs.

"She's in her early twenties, one child and is studying journalism. In her first pageant she placed in the top ten."

"So, she's competed before?" I let out an audible breath. "I could imagine her on the local news. She has that 'professional' look about her."

"Yeah, I see it too," Stacey said. "Lots of women use pageants to kick-start their careers in journalism, politics or even acting. Once she's hired at a local station, she'll never compete again."

"Let's hope she gets hired tonight then." We both laughed.

I finally made it to the front of the line and registered. After they checked my name off the list and handed me my room key, Stacey and I grabbed our overnight bags and headed toward the contestant's wing.

Laughter filled the long hallway. I shivered, feeling the electricity of excitement in the air. We continued to our room, pulling our many bags of luggage behind us. With doors propped open I glanced inside each room to see what was happening. The ladies were taking turns showing their evening gowns to their roommates. Now the laughter sounded forced, nervous, but then, maybe I only imagined it.

Stacey poked me with her elbow and pointed to a large cut-out star, glitzed and taped to the outside of a door, like a Hollywood star in a famous celebrity trailer. Written in bold ink was "Mindy, Mrs. Salem, Oregon."

We stopped, eyes big, staring at each other, and burst into laughter.

"You have got to be kidding!" Stacey clasped a hand over her mouth.

"Who does that?" I gasped for a breath.

"Apparently, she does. That's one for the memory books."

Inside our room, Stacey and I diligently unpacked. We laid out each pair of shoes and hung our wardrobes in the closet. When finished we plopped on the beds and opened our pageant program books.

Stacey fixated on a page, closed her eyes, tilted her head and lifted her chin.

I glanced at her. "What are you doing?"

"Memorizing each judge's name and what they do for a living. Headquarters never releases the names prior to this weekend. That way no lady or their family members can contact a judge before the pageant." She flipped a page. "The judges receive the list of names of contestants and their bio forms weeks before and sign a contract stating they do not personally know any of us."

"What page are you on?" I licked my finger and turned the pages of the spiral-bound book.

"Sixteen. Ask me something about judge number two. We'll study together."

"Okay. I will as soon as I flip through all of these pages, with Mindy's picture."

"What do you mean all?" Stacey's voice rose two full octaves.

~TWENTY-SIX~
Program Book

Stacey frantically turned the pages of the pageant program book to the ad section. "How many pages?" I thought she was going to need a paper bag to breathe.

"Let me turn there again." We counted the pages out loud in unison. "Four, five, six, seven."

"Seven!" Stacey's jaw dropped and her face turned white.

"So, what's the big deal about that?" I shrugged, bored talking about ad pages. I wanted to continue studying each judge's biography.

"What's the big deal? The big deal, each ad page a contestant buys generates revenue for pageant headquarters. Mindy's going to win the director's gift."

"A gift? Nobody told me that." My stomach pinched.

"It's always a beautiful, expensive ring. Last year, it was a ruby." She lowered her gaze at the glossy pages. "It puts my four pages to shame. I really worked hard on those ads, too," she murmured.

"Oh, so headquarters must love her then."

"Yeah, her ad pages paid a lot of the pageant's bills. Don't think for a second the judges aren't going to recognize that. Each ad sends a message to the judges, audience members and the director about whom she knows, who is willing to attach their name to her, who is cheering for her and who she networks with in this state." Stacey's brows drew together looking at Mindy's many ad pages. "Look. A dealership in her city took out a full-page ad supporting her. A local radio station took out a half page ad, and the delegate candidate for Senator of Oregon took out an ad. Crap!" Stacey threw the pageant book against the wall.

"I wonder what my page looks like." I flipped from the bio pages to the ad pages.

"Yours will be the first one. It's in contestant order," Stacey explained.

I looked at my one ad page. "Now, I'm depressed." I slammed the program book closed, and threw it at the wall, just like Stacey had.

We looked at each other and burst out laughing.

"We're acting like babies." I stuck my thumb in my mouth.

"I know, but it's fun. And we are not babies. We're official divas with a capital 'D,'" Stacey added.

I was honored to be part of her diva club, like an insider.

"I know what we can do. Let's pull a Tonya Harding and take her out at the knees," Stacey quipped.

At this I laughed so hard tears ran down my face.

"Lucy," Stacey gasped and pointed at me. "You didn't bring waterproof mascara?"

I jumped off the bed, my heart beating double time at her suggestion. I looked in the mirror which was attached to the dresser, clenched the front, and leaned in closer. "Oh, crumb! This can't be happening, Stacey. What should I do?"

We burst out laughing at my question, as mascara ran down my face.

Stacey pointed at me again, trying to speak through her laughter. "Everyone, who is anyone, knows to bring waterproof mascara to a pageant. That is Basic Diva Rule 101."

There was a rap on the door. We both turned our heads.

"Shhh," Stacey softened her laugh. "They're probably going to tell us to be quiet."

Another knock.

"You answer it," I demanded.

"Yeah, sure, raccoon eyes." Stacey wrinkled her nose like a bunny, crawled off the bed, and opened the door. "Ahh, these must be for Lucy," Stacey told whoever stood at the door. "My husband doesn't buy me rose's anymore." she joked as she shut the door.

"Roses and a gift? For me?" I jumped to snap up the card and read it out loud. "Break a leg! I love you, Lu. Tom."

The roses reminded me of the reason I was here—to compete and win. I cleared room for the large bouquet on the dresser and opened the flat, thin, wrapped gift. It was a personalized license plate, which read, *My Queen*. I explained to Stacey about the car accident, which had happened on the day of my photo shoot right before my surprise birthday party.

"The lady Tom hit would have made a great contestant, if she were married. She was gracious and pretty."

"I understand what you're saying. I look at every woman through pageant eyes, too." Stacey plopped on her bed.

I tapped out a text message to Tom. *Thank U...I miss U...I luv U.* Placing my phone back into my bag, I eagerly returned to the task at hand. Pageant talk with Stacey.

"What does the schedule say tonight's events are?" I stood at the bathroom sink and washed off the black mascara that ran down my cheeks. The cool water was refreshing. I borrowed Stacey's waterproof mascara and reapplied.

"Rehearsal first, then dinner. Afterwards they'll bus us to karaoke. Bring your sneakers," Stacey said.

"Sneakers?" I applied the last coat of black goop to my lashes.

"Yeah, it's opening number rehearsal, which means dance steps."

On the large stage, under the hot lights, all twenty-eight of us stood in four rows of seven, crammed together just like our director's assistant demanded.

It was quiet.

We waited.

Finally, a blonde just over 5' appeared, clipboard in hand, dressed in athletic shorts and a tank top, which showed off her solid body. She looked at each one of us, as if her task were hopeless. "Hello, ladies!" Her voice was deep, unexpected from such a petite lady. "I'm Jenna, your choreographer and captain of the University of Oregon cheerleading team. If you are wondering about my experience, I have plenty. I've studied dance pretty much my whole life."

The ladies clapped for her louder and longer than necessary, in my opinion. Jenna directed us to our positions. Mine was first in the front row. She instructed us where to step, when to turn and how to move our arms, stopping us often to repeat the routine.

During down moments, I tried to gauge who the judges would like most.

The fast learners groaned when the slow learners messed up. My skill level plunked me in the middle.

Surely Stacey would practice with me in our room tonight.

Jenna directed the front row to move to the back every once in a while, showcasing another four ladies, allowing them to have their moment in the spotlight.

"Stop! Stop the music." Jenna yelled to whoever was operating the sound system.

The ladies moaned. Tension mounted between the fast and slow learners. Exhaustion had replaced our excitement.

While Jenna focused on the ladies in the back row, others around me mumbled. I strained to pick out the conversations.

"Within the first five minutes, I picked the top five and I'm one of them," Mindy boasted to a handful of ladies.

I stepped backwards to hear more clearly what they were saying.

"Really? What are your predictions?" Mrs. Bend whispered.

"I'm sure Lily Franklin will take a spot, just because she showed up." Mindy's voice came through harsh and bitter.

Just because she showed up? Stacey would have to explain later.

"Yep, she's in my top five too." the lady behind me added before we broke for dinner.

Returning to the stage I looked to the far corner. A woman sat with her head down, shoulders heaving. *Who was she?* I stepped closer, trying to recognize the hairstyle from the back. *Mrs. Roseburg.*

My list of things to ask Stacey grew.

All of us were tired, and some were grumpy when rehearsal ended. Stacey and I followed the ladies to the elevators, a soft ping sounded and the door glided open.

As soon as we were back in our room, out of earshot of other contestants, I said, "I overheard Mindy say Lily Franklin would make the top five 'just for showing up.' Why did she say that? She sounded so sure of herself." I changed into a pair of black slacks, a shimmery gold tank top, and black high heels. *A perfect karaoke outfit.*

"Well, she's probably right, she will make the top five, but not for the reason Mindy is insinuating. She said that, because Lily is black. Mindy is an idiot and knows no better," Stacey said.

"Ohh, I get it. Her pretty complexion and beautiful hair, coupled with the fact she is a nice, successful woman, doesn't have anything to do with it, huh?" My sarcasm was aimed at Mindy.

~TWENTY-SEVEN~
Karaoke

A full moon hung in the sky, when Stacey and I stepped onto the shuttle. The array of perfume reminded me of where I was and what I was doing. Pageant weekend!

I found an empty seat and scooted to make room for Stacey. Letting out a sigh that the karaoke outing was only two hours long.

A short time later, the driver pulled up to Encore, the pageant program ad said it's a posh, trendy, music inspired karaoke lounge. This should be fun. Spectators flocked around the entrance, looking in our direction. There were whistles and catcalls as we stepped off the bus, one-by-one, wearing banners, tiaras and dressed as if we were attending a Hollywood red carpet event.

A couple of men stood smoking in the corner of the parking lot watching as we walked by. One of the contestants stopped in front of them, pulled her skirt up and dropped into an exaggerated curtsy.

A sour taste rose in my throat at her public display of attention. What made me doubly uncomfortable was how much she loved the attention, and encouraged the men's obvious flirtations.

"It's a married pa…pag…pageant, moron. They're all married," A husky, good-looking man slurred to his pal.

"I don't care. That's even better. They're all ve…very lonely married women. Now, who's the moron?" the man's voice roared. "C'mon, I'm going back inside to watch this. Heck, I might even pop up there on stage and sing a duet with one of them ladies. Are you coming with me?"

"Of course, I am. I'm not missing this."

A soft giggle tickled my throat. The two men trailed behind us, as we entered the dark, noisy lounge. It didn't take us long to fill empty seats at the tables and booths.

Alcohol was ordered and the women hooted and danced around before I'd even set my purse down. Out of pure exhaustion I let out a laugh and my end goal faded away, even if just for a couple of hours. Yet I was certain no one else forgot why we were there, to compete.

From behind the microphone some of the ladies sang 1980s theme songs as others huddled around the karaoke table, filling out forms requesting their songs. Before the night ended, songs ranging from *Abba* to the sound track of *Grease* were sure to be crooned.

Mrs. Geltner glided past, a clipboard in hand. My heart rate tripled, hoping her gaze scanning the room would pass over me.

"Stacey. Stacey, I can't sing." I tugged on her forearm, panic setting in.

"What? What do you mean you can't sing? Everyone can sing." Stacey laughed.

"No, seriously Stacey. I've never karaoked in my life. I mouth the words in church because I'm tone deaf." Sweat beaded on my neck. "What do I do? Help me. I don't want Mrs. Geltner to think I'm a party pooper or that I won't participate in group activities."

"Ree-lax," Stacey said. "I'll tell you what. Let's fill out a form for a group song. You can stand in the middle, lip sync, and blend in. No one will know you can't sing, and you'll look like a team player. How's that for a plan?"

"Oh, thank you, Stacey. That sounds perfect." I relaxed and smiled.

The two drunken men stumbled from table to table, attempting to make small talk with the ladies. They dropped one-liners, trying to engage in a conversation. Stacey and I were next.

"If this bar is a meat market, you must be the filet mignon," one of the men slurred.

"Move along!" Stacey demanded, before they threw down another cheesy pick-up line.

They scooted past.

"Did you see that guy lick his chops like you really were a filet mignon?" I asked through my giggles.

The fresh faced waitress delivered a tray of neon drinks topped with a variety of fruit kabobs to the five ladies at the next table. Her ponytail bounced as she approached us. "Would you like something to drink?" She tapped her foot three times and carried a look on her face that read, "Great, divas."

"I would love a Lemon Drop," Stacey answered.

The waitress took her pen from behind her ear and scribbled something on her order pad.

"And for you?" The waitress waited for my reply.

"Oh, uh…diet pop, please."

I didn't think pageant ladies would drink, because weren't we trying to make a great impression. Again, I was so naïve.

I nudged Stacey with my elbow. "Look at those guys now." I pointed toward the stage, where the drunks were singing their hearts out to "Summer Nights." And doing a good job.

"Tell me more, tell me more. Was it love at first sight?" The crowd joined in.

The waitress brought Stacey her Lemon Drop and my pop. Looking around the room my eyes widened. A fountain of alcohol flowed.

I leaned into Stacey "You're not going to order another Lemon Drop, are you?"

"Oh, no, one is plenty. I'm going to keep my head in the game, even during the down time."

Phew, I'm glad she said that. Not having Courtney, Mom or Tom here, I've been leaning on Stacey to help me through this pageant.

Suddenly, a hollow ache pierced my heart. He should be here with me. I felt like I was leaving him out of a part of my life. I closed my eyes and pressed my fingers to my temples.

A new trio took the stage and I opened my eyes. I focused on the two drunken men welcoming Mindy onto their laps. "Oh, my gosh, Stacey. Look. Over there." Stacey turned around, and we both stared.

"Remind me, Stacey. What kind of a pageant is this?" She shrugged off my question as normal behavior.

"Why is Mindy sprawled out over those guys and running her fingers through their hair?" I wondered if anyone else was shocked. "That's just wrong, just wrong." I pulled my phone out and sent Tom a quick text message, *I miss u! xoxo.*

"Now, where is she going?" Stacey eyes followed Mindy and her admirers. "She can't be going outside with those two men." Stacey craned to see around the people.

"I don't know, but this weekend is growing stranger by the minute." We both laughed.

"It's a subculture all of its own, huh, Lucy?"

Karaoke came to a close. During the ride back to our hotel, a tipsy contestant said loudly, "I just love Demi Moore in the movie *G.I. Jane.*" Everyone giggled, but Stacey and me. I tried to figure out what was so funny.

"How about you, Mindy? Ever watch *G.I. Jane*?" A woman in the front snickered. It was obvious the ladies gossiped about her earlier. It didn't take but a minute, for me to realize what they were laughing about.

'G.I. Mindy' went outside to smoke a cigar with those two men.

I looked at Stacey, to see if she caught on. She did. We burst out laughing.

"Tomorrow, you're going to show up at rehearsal with a shaved head," another lady razzed Mindy. I couldn't believe the ladies would make fun of her, to her face. Liquid courage, I suppose.

"Did you get their digits?" another contestant asked.

"Found a couple of new friends, huh, Mindy?"

Comments flew around the bus.

"Best friends," Mindy waved two fingers crisscrossed, and everyone laughed.

Stacey and I made small talk about the night's events, before we each rolled over and fell asleep. Or, I should say, until she fell asleep.

My mind raced as I reflected on conversations I overheard. If Mindy's predictions were correct, one spot was already taken for Top Five. There still had to be a first, second, third, and fourth runner-up. Might as well be one of them, as long as it wasn't me.

I'm chasing the crown.

~TWENTY-EIGHT~
Pageant Day

Pageant day! I rolled over and stretched. Yesterday, day two of rehearsals, was a blur. Although I barely slept the past two nights, I wasn't the slightest bit tired. If the flow of energy could be seen, it would look like magnetic swirls of neon colors. I was amazed to discover that a person could go without sleep for two days and two nights and still function and think.

As the first rays of sun streaked through the crack in the curtains, I tiptoed passed Stacey to the shower. The three-hour preparation time needed for private interviews had begun. By the time I wrapped a towel around myself, Stacey had awakened and took my place in the bathroom. Once we were both dressed, we practiced interview questions as she applied makeup and I fixed my hair. Stacey's answers were intelligent and precise, polished and perfect.

I studied her answers and gleaned ideas. Then it was my turn.

"Where do you see yourself in five years?" Stacey picked up her lip liner.

"I plan to volunteer with young children, who need help with their speech and—"

Stacey pointed at the clock. "It's time. We need to go upstairs to the interview room."

We gathered our suitcases, full of wardrobe changes, extra shoes, makeup, and accessories, to take with us later for the pageant tonight. We walked down the long dimly, lit hallway to the elevator. I stood tall, firmly planting each step on the carpet without a wobble.

We joined the other contestants in the holding room. The pageant staff whipped back and forth in organized chaos from the room where we waited, to the interview room across the hall. Clipboards in hand, the staff kept us on time for our private interviews. We stared at the closed door, waiting for our turns to enter the room where the judges were.

The electricity, which flowed in the air earlier that morning, was now grounded. It became eerily quiet. For the first time, since drawing my white ball I was glad to be contestant number one. My interviews would start right away, and I wouldn't have to sit with the other contestants eyeing the closed door. The pressure of waiting would have surely turned my fair skin beet red.

A staff member appeared and announced that the judges were ready to begin the interviews. Adrenalin speared me when my name was called, along with contestants two, three, four, and five. We stood in unison and entered through the double doors. From behind me, I heard Stacey say, "Good luck," to all five of us.

In the banquet room the five distinguished judges, each at their own desk, were placed in a half-moon layout, similar to the day at the school when Courtney and I rehearsed with Mr. Baker, Ms. Larson, and Becky.

We stood by the entrance and waited. The bell jingled and I walked confidently to the judge who appeared to be in her mid-fifties and stood behind desk number one, made eye contact and shook her hand. She returned my smile, with an inviting one that encouraged me to maintain my confidence.

Calmness blossomed from a place deep within. I waited until she sat down, then did the same, sitting as Courtney had coached me. Erect, crossed ankles to the side, hands in my lap with palms up.

"Hello, Lucy." The judge gazed over her reading glasses at me. "Tell me how would you explain to other women that competing in a pageant is a good experience in today's society?"

No small talk. No warm up questions. No pauses. I sorted through my memory, like a Rolodex, flipping in fast motion, trying to remember her bio in the pageant book. I didn't want to offend her if she was an activist for women's rights, or if she believed in traditional, old-fashioned ways. *Remember. Remember.* I willed myself but my mind remained blank. In that moment, I decided to be true to my beliefs and convictions, and hope the judge would respect my honesty.

In a twisted way, I was now glad Samantha and I had that uncomfortable conversation about a woman's role in society. As awkward and upset as I was with the topic at the time, I realized it had prepared me for this question.

"A pageant recognizes women's influence and gives women a voice that may not be otherwise heard. That voice can say, 'We, as women, are important and worthy of equal rights. We are beautiful ladies, well-educated, disciplined, and goal-oriented. But most importantly, we are not just decorations.' When we do showcase our beauty, both inner and outer, we continue to work on that path of equality." I thought my answer came out jumbled and I hoped the judge didn't notice.

The judge nodded her head, her stare softening. I relaxed, and was able to talk confidently with the other four judges.

After my private interviews, I took the elevator up to the room, while I came down from an adrenaline high. I plopped on the end of the bed with the television remote and flipped through the channels. Restless, I paced, then crumpled onto the bed again. Time dragged as I waited for Stacey to finish her interviews so we could compare notes.

Just when I thought I couldn't wait any longer the door to our room opened and Stacey walked in, her expression relaxed. She looked as if she'd just come back from a restful afternoon, sitting under an oak tree reading her favorite book. She walked straight past me to her purse, but didn't say a word, not one word.

"How were your interviews?" I asked, just above a whisper.

She didn't answer. Instead, she rummaged through her cute, delicate bag, pulled out two king-sized chocolate bars and unwrapped one as fast as she could.

"What are you doing?" I stood with my hand over my mouth. Her hurried actions contradicted her calm features.

She extended the other candy bar toward me while stuffing a large piece of chocolate into her mouth with her other hand. "What do you think I'm doing? I'm indulging." Chocolate spilled out of her mouth. It smelled delicious. "Chocolate, it's my reward once the interview portion of competition is over. It calms me down."

"But…but, what about your weight?"

"If I gain a pound, it will show up tomorrow, not tonight." She collapsed on her bed like a rag doll.

Makes sense to me.

I opened the candy bar and we each took a series of small, quick ceremonial bites in silence.

"Mmm, thanks. I needed that." I licked the last of the chocolate from my front teeth.

I was blessed to have Stacey, a friend who could bond over chocolate.

"I've been starving myself for a month now." She devoured her last piece. "Time to celebrate. Interviews are over."

We discussed our interview questions and answers, trying to figure out how well we did and what the judges might think of us. After we had exhausted the topic, we turned our attention to the news in case our 'on-stage' question later that evening might be related to current events.

~

Stacey and I stepped into a cloud of aroma from hairsprays, lotions, and potions. In the crowded dressing area, heat waved from the lighted makeup mirrors lining the length of the wall.

I paused, took in a deep breath, closed my eyes and stamped into my memory forever the smells and feelings of such a special night.

I stepped over strapless bras and nylons, strewn all over the floor, careful not to twist my ankle on the high heels peeking out from beneath the small piles.

Five ladies flitted around the cramped dressing room I didn't recognize. They wore nametags, with "Dressers" in bold script. They hustled from contestant to contestant, zipping up dresses, fastening snaps, and buttoning buttons. When I needed the help of a dresser to zip my evening gown, I squeezed in line to grab the attention of one of them. Once zipped, I fought my way to the line for the makeup artist and hairstylist for final touches.

The room bustled with activity, but the chaos had order. There was a peculiar quiet throughout the room with the exception of a burst of whispers every few minutes.

I concentrated on which accessory went with this wardrobe, and kept an eye on my competition. Bright colors edged my vision as ladies unzipped their plastic wardrobe bags and the contents spilled out like a tidal wave of seashells scattered on a beach.

"Ladies, two minutes till the opening number!" A stage manager rushed in. "Two minutes!"

We dropped our combs, makeup brushes, and lipsticks and rushed to line up at the stage entrance.

"Lucy Rupp, right?" The stage manager with a clipboard asked, as I stood at the front of the line. I nodded, my heart lurched, then spiraled to my french tipped toes, forced to go on stage first.

The lights dimmed, we marched single-file behind the closed curtain and found our places on stage. We waited in position, arms outstretched down and hands opened. The synthetic fog rolled across the stage, the music swelled as the curtains opened.

The audience applauded, and shouted names of their favorite contestants. The cacophony reminded me of an auction house. Darkness crept around the spotlights, blinding my vision, allowing me to concentrate on my dance steps.

After the longest 150 seconds of my life, the song stopped. We stood, hands in air with contestant smiles, as the curtains closed with a swish. I almost couldn't contain my laughter. I made it through the dance remembering the choreographer's instructions. We shuffled off stage as fast as we could to change for the next segment, fitness.

There I was, standing on stage again behind the curtain, only this time, alone. I took a deep breath, sucked in my stomach, and waited for the Emcee to finish describing in detail the next phase of competition to the audience.

The Emcee's voice boomed, as the curtains opened. "Our first contestant this evening is…Mrs. Springfield…Lucy Rupp." The Emcee's voice boomed, as the curtains opened. His voice grew louder as he emphasized my name, just like Ed McMahon announced Johnny Carson.

I used the entire stage, as I walked a figure-eight formation to model my official black unitard. The Co-Emcee read my scripted facts. "Lucy is a homemaker, with three beautiful children. She recently had an addition to their family, a cat, named Tuxedo."

The audience ahhed and I grinned on the inside. The Co-Emcee continued, "To stay in shape, Lucy enjoys running, weight-lifting, and riding her bike with her husband and children."

A camera light flashed in my eyes. I blinked twice in rapid succession but refused to squint.

"Don't be plastic, *be faaantastic*."

I recognized that voice and relief spread through my veins. I thought about the day Dusty Joe took my headshot in his studio. He said I had the whole package, the *winning package*. I was leaning on those words now.

"Nice job," he whispered, under the Emcee's voice. "You look maaarvelous."

"Go, Lucy!" Julie whooped from the crowd. My smile grew.

"Go, Springfield!" The men in The Gang yelled.

My eyes finally adjusted to the darkness. My kids sat in a reserved section holding signs. *"Team Lucy."* Even Mr. Baker, Ms. Larson, and Becky each held a poster board. Julie must have been in charge of the Lucy signs. Sitting next to Colleen, Samantha grinned as she held a big poster, *"Mrs. Springfield is the best."*

I glanced at the first two rows, the husband's section. My heart melted. Tom, handsome in his tuxedo, biting a nail.

My section continued to scream and shout, "Go, Mom....Go, Lucy....Go, Mrs. Springfield!"

As I performed another pass-by on the stage, a loud whistle pierced the hall. I surveyed the audience, spying Claudia, her fingers in her mouth, the only one standing. Looking back over my shoulder in her direction, my eyes locked with hers as I mouthed, "Thank you."

I exited the stage to the Emcee saying, "Thank you contestant number one! Lucy Rupp!"

Dashing to the dressing room, I wondered if the time spent on the treadmill, lifting weights, and denying myself ice cream and donuts had been worth it. And, to what end? This moment? This *forty-five second* moment? The judges' scores would be my answer.

Backstage I peeled off my tight aerobic outfit and dressed for the next segment. I paused to soak in the moment, once again.

Stacey stood nearby, adjusting her unitard. "Stacey?" She turned to me. Finally, I had a chance to repay her for all the tips she'd given me. "When you go on stage, Dusty Joe is on your right taking pictures. I thought you'd like to know, so you're not caught off guard by the camera flashes."

"Thanks, Lu. I appreciate the heads up."

I had a feeling she already knew he was there and humored me, just to let me think I had shared some great revelation with her.

"What? Dusty Joe is out there?" Mindy butted into our conversation. It was the first time she had acknowledged me.

If she was eavesdropping on Stacey and me, *maybe she thought I was competition for her after all.*

"Why headquarters allowed him to be the professional photographer of this pageant is beyond me. It's embarrassing." Mindy shook her head in disapproval, her lacquered hair not moving an inch in the process.

Nobody said a word while zipping and buttoning and changing and getting ready for the evening gown competition, but we all knew what she meant. She moved away and I sighed in relief.

Stacey rolled her eyes. "Remind me not to vote for her as Mrs. Congeniality."

I gave her a smirk, then focused on transforming from athletic to runway gorgeous.

A designated pageant dresser hooked the straps on the back of my evening gown, and I tucked my gel-filled enhancements into my strapless bra. I didn't want to use duct tape to lift my breasts after Mrs. Geltner warned us against it based on personal experience. She had told us, "Never wrap duct tape around your torso. Use athletic tape, because, when you rip off the tape, you will scar yourself permanently." To prove her point, she lifted her blouse and revealed a scar around her rib cage. Everyone there let out an 'oooh.'

As ready as I'd ever be, I swirled around, looking in the mirror. Beautiful, confident, strong, powerful. Of course, wearing red helped. A stylist completed the final touches on my up-do hairstyle and stuck sparkly bobby pins around in my hair.

A hush dropped over the dressing room, the ladies around me stopped what they were doing and stared at me for several seconds.

A nervous laugh bubbled from my throat "What? Did I forget something?" I asked the ladies. My palms sweated, and I wrung my hands together.

"No." Lily answered, mascara wand in hand. "You…you just look gorgeous!"

The other contestants nodded in agreement. Their wide eyes moved from the top of my head to my heels, then back up.

"Thank you." I stood straighter and beamed. Their reaction to my red, glitzy evening gown boosted my confidence even more. I was ready to step in front of the audience.

Once again on stage, behind the closed curtain, I placed my left foot in the ten o'clock position, and my right foot in the twelve o'clock position, knee slightly bent, just as Courtney had instructed me. I held my shoulders back, my arms hung loosely by my sides. I made a 'C' curve, by bending my arms at the elbows. My fingers were relaxed, but held together. Courtney's voice ran through my mind. "No pointer finger like a gun." One last exhale and a big smile. Soft classical music began. The Emcee's deep, professional voice with a hint of gentleness filled the auditorium to match the elegance of the evening gown portion of the show.

"To begin the evening gown competition, let us again revisit Mrs. Springfield, Lucy Rupp." The Emcee's voice with a hint of gentleness filled the auditorium to match the elegance of the evening gown portion of the show.

The curtains opened slowly and the spotlight beamed on back center stage. The synthetic fog rose, wrapping itself around my perfectly poised stance in my red sparkling evening gown against the midnight black backdrop.

Loud gasps fanned across the audience, followed by a hush, then thunderous applause. I held onto my bright red lipstick smile as the unexpected reaction from the audience continued to roll over me.

This is what a queen feels like.

My head high, I walked gracefully to mid-center stage where Tom waited, with a red rose. He handed me the flower, his nervousness visible by the way his Adam's apple rolled. He kissed me on the cheek, looped his arm through mine, and escorted me to front-center stage.

"You're beautiful." He whispered with a shine in his eyes. He unhooked his arm from mine, releasing me to model my gown down the illuminated runway. He stood straight and tall, hands behind his back, as he watched me work the stage.

Soft compliments rose from the audience as I walked past. After my Grace Kelly moment on the runway, I returned to Tom.

Tom smiled at me, the way he did the first time he'd seen me walk down the hall in high school. He looped his arm back in mine. "You are my queen. I love you," he said softly as he escorted me off the stage. He exited to the left, while I exited to the right. "You are my hero," I said, under my breath, but with the backstage clatter, he didn't hear me.

~TWENTY-NINE~
Top Ten

Time stopped. The moment had come for the Emcee to announce the top ten. If my name wasn't called this would be the end of my journey.

My toes, jammed in my high heels, ached. My bangs stuck to my forehead. My hands were moist and I wanted to wipe them, but on what? I couldn't breathe. I waited. We waited.

Finally, the Emcee spoke. I pleaded to the pageant gods. *Please let me be in the top ten.*

"Ladies, are you ready to hear who will advance to the top ten?" The Emcee tossed us an easy grin. He spun on his heels with high energy and in a controlled shout, "Audience! Are you ready to hear, who will advance?"

The Emcee brought an aura of intensity to the auditorium that stirred excitement in the audience, and held the contestant's emotions, wishes, and dreams in his voice.

We kept enormous smiles, all forced. Yes, we were ready.

"When I call your name, please take a step forward." He commanded. "I will announce the top ten in random order, which has no significance on your scores." My heart thumped. One by one he announced the contestants' names. "The first lady to advance is…Holly Nelson, Mrs. Grants Pass."

The audience clapped.

The Emcee paused. "Carrie Campbell, Mrs. Ashland."

The applause grew louder.

"Lily Franklin, Mrs. Clackamas."

The audience rose to their feet, cheering.

"The next lady to make top ten is…Stacey Smith, Mrs. Portland." I wanted to run and hug her but instead I clapped extra hard.

"Rounding out the half way mark…Mindy Storm, Mrs. Salem."

A flu-like feeling settled in the pit of my stomach, and my ears hummed a dull tone for a few seconds. The Emcee had already announced over half of the top ten. Mrs. Bend and Mrs. Roseburg joined the ladies in the new half-moon circle in front of us. I zoned out in a fog of worry.

Then, after what seemed like forever, the words, "Number ten, Mrs. Springfield, Lucy Rupp!" echoed. I shut my eyes and let the tension escape from my neck and shoulders. My body melted with relief. I hugged Mrs. Redmond, who stood next to me, a little too long. I took a step forward. My family and friends' cheered over the crowd. My gaze met Stacey's. We smiled at each other with understanding. I looked up and down the new row, as gossiped at rehearsal I stood with Mindy, Stacey, Holly, Lily, and Carrie.

After the applause died down, the Emcee called for a fifteen-minute intermission. Off stage my heart leaped, I located Stacey, squeezed her, and we jumped up and down, like high school girls who had been chosen for the cheerleading team.

In the dressing room, my heart plummeted. In one corner, the ladies who didn't make the top ten huddled in a group-hug, crying, their pain wafted off them like cheap cologne. The atmosphere was heavy and thick, like dairy cream. Instinctively, I slowed my pace and took measured steps toward my spot in the room.

My gaze shifted, not wanting them to see me looking. Of course, they would be upset. I knew rejection from the judges would hurt. Those of us who made top ten did our best to contain our gregarious smiles and overly congratulatory statements.

I am sure no one wanted to further hurt their feelings. Everyone except Mindy who paraded like a peacock with beautiful feathers all fanned out. I wanted to pull her perfect hair out of her perfect hair-do.

I wasn't sure if there was proper pageant etiquette to follow or not. I was glad it wasn't me standing in the corner crying. Observing the slumped huddle, sadness seared my heart. I did what I would want any other contestant to do for me. I gave each a hug, and told them what a great job they did, regardless of where they placed. Stacey and Lily followed my lead.

Dark whispers traveled around the room led by Mindy, solidifying I made the right decision to approach them. Not prepared for the harsh reality of this emotional component, I watched Mindy, turn side to side in the mirror, studying her outfit. She wore a smug smile, too consumed with her own admiration to come over and console the other ladies.

I retouched my hair and checked my makeup one more time, before returning for the on-stage question. I looked at my nails. If they weren't acrylic I would have bitten them down to the quick.

I waited backstage for the Emcee to call my name. *What if* my bad dream comes true? *What if* my mind goes blank and not a word comes out of my mouth? *What if* I don't know the answer to the question? *What if* I mispronounce a word? *What if* I trip over a political landmine? These thoughts were interrupted, when my name was announced and I walked to center stage.

Smiling, I stood near the Emcee, knees trembling, resisting the urge to grab him for support. He talked with me before pulling a piece of folded paper from the infamous fishbowl with my question. The casual visit gave me a chance, to quiet my mind, relax my body, and find my voice.

I held my breath waiting for him to read from the thin, oblong sheet of paper.

"Lucy, what made you decide to enter the Mrs. Oregon pageant?"

My stomach knotted.

That was it. That was my question. That was the question from the fish bowl. No, how to save the world, or fix poverty. No, controversial questions about same sex marriages, pro-choice or pro-life.

For goodness sake, ask me about world peace.

No, my question was, what made you decide to enter the Mrs. Oregon pageant. It was too easy. My nervous knot twisted tighter. I couldn't have heard him right. Maybe the small talk portion hadn't ended after all. No, I had seen him reach into the fish bowl and retrieve the question.

"I'm sorry, could you repeat the question?"

"Certainly. What made you decide to enter the Mrs. Oregon pageant?"

My mind scrambled with how to answer and not sound vain but intelligent, important, and someone with a cause. Aware that too much time passed, I opened my mouth and let my heart speak.

"I entered the pageant to be a role model for my daughter and for married women across America. I entered to prove, that by competing, you don't have to set the feminist movement back twenty years." I took a breath and smiled, the words coming easier.

"Instead, I hope to show other ladies, that with hard work, dedication, and commitment, you can accomplish your goals and dreams. As women, we can do whatever we set our minds to, and no one can stop us." I could see nods in the audience as my words connected.

With more confidence I continued. "Entering opened doors for me that would not have opened if I hadn't decided to join the Mrs. Oregon pageant. I've met new friends, learned how to apply makeup, gained communication skills, and best yet, lost fifteen pounds."

With that, the audience released a collective breath, and gave me an enthusiastic applause. Most women in the audience would relate to the honesty of my answer.

"Thank you, Lucy. Everyone, give Mrs. Springfield another round of applause." The clapping and cheers erupted as I exited the stage. I stopped, in the darkness behind the curtain to listen, one more time, to the crowd's support.

My big night was over. Nothing more I could do, but wait. Nothing I could change. My red dress would stay red. My high heels would still hurt my feet, and I still couldn't pronounce many of the words others took for granted. But, I knew who I was inside, no matter what the judges' scores told me. I was Lucy Rupp, wife, mother, and beautiful inside and out, with an inner confidence no one could steal from me.

The pageant swirled into its Grand Finale with the introduction of Keene Curtis, to serenade the audience while the judges and auditor tallied the score sheets.

Curtis strode onto the stage in a tuxedo with tails. With a confident posture he created instant rapport with the audience in one flash of a smile and sang, "The Anchor Holds." The lyrics piercing my heart as he continued.

My marriage would survive. My kids learned I would always be there for them. My morals stayed intact. I overcame obstacles that had once made me fearful and insecure. A tear wet my cheek, proud of my emotional and physical accomplishments.

All twenty-eight of us stood behind the stage curtain, for the last time. The final lyrics resonated from Keene Curtis, and the crowd was up on their feet, with a roar of applause.

~THIRTY~
The Crown

The Emcee's words reached us as we stood behind the curtain. "Ladies and gentleman, the time everyone has been waiting for…." He took a deep breath. "To find out who will be your next, Mrs. Oregon."

The curtains opened and my pulse rate climbed. Our husband's stood on X's, taped to the floor, just like they were taught in the husbands' rehearsal.

"Prior to announcing the winner, we have a few awards to present." We would have to wait longer to hear who would be the new Mrs. Oregon.

The crowd sighed, but it was nothing like my deflation. The crowd's response turned into an electric energy that traveled throughout the room.

"The first award is Mrs. Photogenic. A panel of judges and staff at pageant headquarters decides who receives this award," said the Emcee. "*And,* Mrs. Photogenic goes to…Mrs. Springfield, Lucy Rupp!"

My heart raced. A roar of whistling, whooping and hollering filled my ears as the audience cheered with my reserved section of family and friends, who raised their signs and waved them in the air.

I stepped forward to accept my award then paused as Dusty Joe focused his lens and snapped my picture. He gave me a thumbs up. I beamed, proud that it was his photo, which helped me win the prize. I stepped back in line. My confidence inflated like a helium balloon, my belief of winning with it.

"The second award tonight is Mrs. Congeniality. Earlier today, the contestants voted on who showed good sportsmanship, leadership and who was the friendliest throughout the pageant weekend. This award goes to…Stacey Smith, Mrs. Portland!"

I chuckled. Stacey had not wanted Mrs. Congeniality. An inside joke among contestants, had attached an unofficial stigma to it. The award was a token fat ladies award, a sympathy vote for the contestant that no one believed would win the pageant.

Of course, she won Mrs. Congeniality she was the nicest lady here, and I was blessed to have her as my friend. She deserved it.

Stacey graciously stepped forward, accepted her award, turned around and thanked the ladies for voting for her, and blew us kisses. She looked at me. Her expression told me, *Oh crap.*

I mouthed, *I'm sorry.*

She took a step back into her place on stage.

"The results are in," the Emcee announced. The crowd quieted, waiting for him to receive the sealed envelope.

This was it, the moment I had worked so hard for the past nine months. I wanted to win. I had to win. Everything slowed—the Emcee's actions, the crowd's clapping, and my heartbeat.

I searched past the bright lights and located Dad holding Suzy so she could see over the crowd. Jake and Adam stood on their chairs next to Mom. The Gang, Claudia, Samantha, Courtney with Mr. Baker, Ms. Larson, and Becky all sat on the edge of their seats. Even Mrs. Abernathy. I wanted to make them proud, and prove to the naysayers that I was worthy to be Mrs. Oregon.

On stage, the husbands stood behind us. We clutched each other's hands and waited for the announcement that would change one of our lives. This time, I didn't want to hear my name until the Emcee announced the winner at the end.

The Emcee opened the envelope very slowly and pulled out a white card. "Let's begin. Fourth runner-up in the Mrs. Oregon pageant is..."

Please don't announce my name. Anyone but me.

"Mrs. Clackamas, Lily Franklin!"

The crowd clapped and cheered. Lily smiled, but her eyes told a different story. She stepped forward without hesitation. Mrs. Geltner met her on stage, handing her a plaque and bouquet of flowers, then handed Lily's husband a tiara. With trembling hands, he placed it on top of Lily's head.

The moment the tiara settled into place, Dusty Joe slipped unobtrusively from the side curtain and snapped photos of Lily, with her husband and Mrs. Geltner. Then, Lily returned to her spot on stage.

"Third runner-up Mrs. Portland, Stacey Smith!"

Mrs. Portland's body jolted as if the Emcee's voice had touched her with an electrical current. The look of disappointment on Stacey's face was obvious, even though she tried to hide it behind her huge smile and extra white teeth.

Mrs. Geltner hurried onto the stage with a tiara plaque and roses. Again with the tiara settled Dusty Joe photographed Stacey.

My name hadn't been called, yet. Every perfect pageant hair on my scalp prickled. I could be the winner.

"And second runner-up…Mrs. Grants Pass, Holly Nelson!"

Holly? Ohhh, the sleeper Stacey told me about. I'd forgotten all about her.

I looked at Stacey, and she rolled her eyes.

"We're getting closer ladies. Now the first runner-up has the responsibility to take over the queen's duties, if something should happen to the queen during her reign." The Emcee paused.

I sneaked a peek at the remaining ladies, which included Mindy and Carrie Campbell. Panic grabbed my heart and wouldn't let go. Maybe I hadn't even made the Top Five. A thousand butterflies tangoed in my stomach.

"The first runner-up issss, Mrs. Ashland, Carrie Campbell!"

Only six contestants left, including Mindy.

She couldn't have won. She's mean. I'm nice. Surely the judges could see the differences.

My smile froze and my eyes blurred with a sudden rush of tears. It's her or me. I forced down the emotions that threatened to overflow.

A drum roll rumbled in the background. The Emcee turned toward the ladies whose names hadn't been called and smiled.

I took a deep breath, pulled my shoulders back, and looked into the crowd where my family and friends stood. My heart swelled and I knew right then the meaning of *true* beauty. Faith. Hope. Love. *True Inner Beauty.*

I stared at Mindy Storm dazzled and poised, not a worry on her face.

"And your new queen is…" The Emcee's voice thundered as the crowd hushed. "Mrs. Salem, Mindy Storm!"

The crowd broke into applause and whistles.

I slow-clapped and smiled, hoping the edges of disappointment flooding my heart didn't show.

Mindy buried her face in shaky hands for a second. Then, she extended her hand toward the judges in a poignant gesture of gratitude, a response I am sure she had rehearsed a million times.

I wasn't even in the running.

What went wrong, I'm not in the top five? I'm not part of the coronation court.

All I wanted to do was run home, pull on my sweats, crawl into bed and disappear for days. I had to face my husband, family, and friends with no crown.

The remaining ladies of the top ten continued to stand, while Mindy's cheating husband lovingly placed the sparkling crown on her head. It glistened like snowflakes in her hair. He laid the bouquet of flowers into her arms.

Mrs. Geltner draped a floor-length mink coat around her shoulders, and whispered into her ear. Mindy then glided across the stage and down the runway in a full Queen's walk.

The Emcee again proclaimed, "Ladies and gentleman...meet your new Mrs. Oregon!"

The crowd went crazy.

She waved and smiled at the cheering audience. Ripples of applause spread through an auditorium filled with smiling faces. Photographers surged forward to capture the scene, and hundreds of flashes from the audience cameras sent waves of light throughout the room. My tears, threatened to fall. Soon, I would have private time backstage.

Mindy finished her Queen's walk. We all huddled around her to hug and leave lipstick prints on her cheek. Dusty Joe circled us with his camera, and the other contestants flooded onto the stage to congratulate the top four...and Mindy.

In the middle of the commotion, I stepped forward and made eye contact with her. "Congratulations, Mindy. Well done." I forced a smile and hid my disappointment. I needed to talk to Stacey.

Once behind the curtain, I watched Stacey position herself for the traditional photos of the top four, with the Queen. At this point, I would have been happy being in the top five. I couldn't stand there and watch any longer.

I retreated to the dressing room and waited for Stacey to join me. I stuffed my makeup, shoes, jewelry, and clothes into my bag. I was exhausted, quiet, sad.

Stacey approached me from behind. "I'm sorry, you didn't win, Lucy."

"I'm sorry that you didn't win." I embraced her.

Stacey sighed "You know what they say? 'A different night, different judges, a different winner.'"

I nodded and continued to pack. The glow of winning slipped away and I couldn't keep the disappointment at bay much longer.

"You never know why a judge scores the way they do. It may have nothing to do with you. It could be all about them. Maybe you reminded a judge of someone they didn't like." Stacey zipped her cosmetic bag. "Your red hair could remind them of an ex-wife, or a crazy co-worker who went postal. You never know."

"But all my hard work, all the money I spent, what I put Tom through." A sob escaped and jolted my ribs. I sank against the back of a chair. "Was it worth it? Really? For what? So, I could have my glory moment on stage for five minutes?" Pain seared my heart and a steady stream of tears fell.

"Come on, Lucy. Yes, it's worth it." Stacey handed me a tissue. "You may not know why now, but pageants change women. They open doors. They are vehicles to build self-esteem and confidence." She placed her hand on my back. "The experience in front of crowds stays with you. And, if you ever need to interview for a job, you'll knock it out of the ballpark."

The stagehands streamed into the dressing room, interrupting our conversation. They seemed oblivious to the mood in the room.

"You're right. I'm just tired. I haven't slept for a couple of days." I sighed.

"I know, but we need to make our appearance at the Queen's Ball. Now let's hurry before the champagne and hors d' oeuvres are gone."

~THIRTY-ONE~
I'll Always Have My Memories

I huffed on the treadmill, pushing myself to complete the workout as strongly as I had started it. The pageant seemed like a lifetime ago, not a mere four weeks. Tom and I tried to return to life pre-pageant, but the rhythm changed. I continued to work my home business selling scrapbook supplies. In my closet hung expensive clothes I might never wear again, but I had a great figure, and a renewed confidence.

"Looking good, Lucy." Tom strolled into the office and pulled his real estate files from the cabinet.

"Thanks, babe. I want to keep the weight off." I said, breathed deeply between each word. I stepped off the treadmill. "Hey, at least the treadmill will be used."

"I'm glad the birthday gift is still appreciated."

"What's that in your hand?" I motioned to the brown box.

He shrugged. "It came in the mail today addressed to you." I took the box and opened it pulling out a thank you card and a framed picture.

"It's from headquarters." I ran my finger along the edge of the frame. "A picture of us on stage." Dusty Joe had captured the perfect moment, beautifully, Tom handing me the red rose. It wasn't a poster-sized portrait, like the one Courtney showcased of her with the crown, but our picture captured the love between us.

"May I?" Tom studied the photo. "I'm still not used to your hair color." He shook his head and handed the photo back.

I touched my dark brown hair. "Do ya like it?" I purposely arched one eyebrow, feistiness in my voice.

"It's different all right, but sexy," he teased, pausing in the doorway.

"I'm going to grow it long. Real long."

The phone rang, interrupting our conversation. Tom answered, handed me the phone, pecked my cheek and whispered "It's Stacey, I'll go check on the kids."

"Stacey. Oh, my gosh. How are you?" I screamed.

"Fine. Fine," she answered. She rushed past the small talk and dived straight into the gossip. "Did you hear?"

"Hear what?" I wiped my face with a towel.

"About Mindy."

"No. What about her?" I asked.

"Her husband filed for divorce. He left her for another woman."

I almost dropped the phone. "Wow! Are you serious?"

"Pageant headquarters took the crown away from her today. You know what that means? First runner-up, Carrie Campbell, is now Queen." I imagined Stacey wearing a wicked sneer knowing Carrie would not be eligible to compete next year.

"I'm in shock right now. And you sound a little too cheery, Ms. Stacey."

"She had no business competing in the first place. She knew her marriage was in trouble. She did it for the publicity, to advance her career. I don't feel bad for her." Stacey added.

"I see your point." My voice lowered. "It's just sad. She should have spent the time and energy she invested into winning the pageant into her marriage."

Stacey and I chatted about each lady we had competed against, and what they were doing now. It felt good to be an official member of the pageant club.

I told Stacey about planning to grow my hair long and changing the color. Stacey told me she had a few nips and tucks scheduled on her calendar.

Of course, she did.

"Are you competing next year?" Stacey asked. Before I answered she continued, "I am. I already submitted my paperwork. You remember the four-year plan." She chuckled.

"According to your plan, you will win. So, why would I enter?" We giggled. "No, I don't think I'll compete next year, but I'll be there to cheer you on. I promise."

"Lucy, you have to compete. It won't be any fun without you." She whined, and then we laughed. "You're my roomie."

"No Stace, I'm going to try something different."

A deep rasp came from behind me. "Ahem." I turned my head and grinned at Tom who stood in the doorway.

"Gotta go, Stacey. Thanks for calling. I'll talk to you later." I said real fast then hung up. "How long have you been standing there?" I widened my stance and put a hand on my hip.

"Long enough. You're up to something, Lucy." He gave me a suspicious look. "What roller coaster ride are you going to take this family on now?"

"Meee?" I fluttered my eyelashes and slapped my hand to my chest.

"Out with it Luc."

I gave Tom an innocent smile. "I've applied to a reality television show!"

Made in the USA
San Bernardino, CA
11 October 2013